The
Shooting

The Shooting

The Impact Series

C K Westbrook

4 Horsemen
Publications, Inc.

4 Horsemen
Publications, Inc.

4 Horsemen Publications, Inc.
1497 Main St. Suite 169
Dunedin, FL 34698
4horsemenpublications.com
info@4horsemenpublications.com

Cover by Jen Kotick
Typesetting by Niki Tantillo
Edited by Heather Teele

Library of Congress Control Number: 2022931321

Paperback ISBN-13: 978-1-64450-497-0
Hardcover ISBN-13: 978-1-64450-552-6
EBook ISBN-13: 978-1-64450-496-3
Audiobook ISBN-13: 978-1-64450-495-6

For Talisker and Ray

ACKNOWLEDGEMENTS:

I want to thank 4 Horsemen Publications for taking a chance on me and this novel. This work of fiction would not exist without the fantastic editing skills, knowledge, support, and friendship of Chelsea. Nor would it exist without my early (and patient) readers, Denise and Nicholas, or my sisters, Shana and Jess, for their constant moral support, advice, and technical help. I am grateful to Lynn for her brilliant expertise and advice. I also want to thank my silent writing partners that were with me from page one to the end, Skye and Talisker. My most profound gratitude and appreciation is for Jeffrey, for his constant support and encouragement of all my crazy adventures, including writing this novel.

Table of Contents

ONE

The Shooting

Kate was running along her favorite trail near the creek where the water was low and still from lack of rain. While the D.C. weather was hot and sunny, the trail provided some shade. Unlike the day before when crippling anxious thoughts took over during her run, today Kate tried to channel peace and let herself feel free.

"There is nothing I can do about anything, so I refuse to worry and be sad," she mumbled to herself through her bright green bandana mask.

Just breathe and appreciate the green woods, beautiful trees, and singing birds, Kate thought. She waved cheerfully to fellow runners and dog walkers. Few people waved back. The virus seemed to take away people's desire to be polite, but Kate kept waving and smiling with her eyes.

As she reached the exact place where she'd been overcome with anxiety the day before, Kate's heart started to race. *Not today, anxiety. You got this, Kate. You just need a good song.* She paused to change her music on her old iPod and was scrolling for a good playlist when she heard an explosion.

What the hell?

She clasped her hands over her ears and squatted down, trying to get low, like shooting drills always recommended. As shots went off like firecrackers, she channeled her breath and stared at the ground, preparing to be hit by something.

Lifting her eyes just enough, she tried to assess the scene. *What is causing the explosions? What is all the popping? Did a nearby transmission box blow up? A series of car bombs? Has the President's army of racist misogynists made good on their threat to take over the city?*

She scanned around her for other runners on the trail but seemed all alone. The flight or fight instinct took over, but she didn't know who to fight or in what direction to run.

The explosions persisted, like hundreds of cars backfiring at the same time. Or fireworks, which were harmful to wildlife. She hated them. She looked around, her hands still covering her ears to soften the sharp, harsh sounds to no avail. Some of the pops seemed close, like just through the woods or across the creek, and others sounded far off, like fireworks downtown near the monuments.

Another runner came around the bend, heading toward Kate.

"Run!" she yelled, flying past Kate.

"Where?" Kate yelled back. "What is it?" she yelled to the runner's back, but the runner did not slow down to answer.

As fast as the cracks, pops, and explosions started, they slowed down.

She had to get home.

Sweating, breathless, Kate started running as fast as she could for the row house she and Kyle rented together. A few "after pops" went off, making Kate jump every time. They came with less and less frequency—like the last popcorn kernels at the end of the bag in a microwave. Some still sounded so close that she flinched. Others made her look in different directions to see if she could identify what was making all the racket.

Finally home, she flew up the stairs and tried to put her key in the lock, but her hands were shaking. She didn't look behind her, afraid an explosion would go off on the porch.

Kyle opened the door, pulled Kate inside, and slammed it closed behind her.

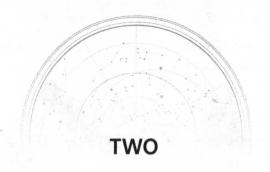

TWO

The Shooting

Kyle pulled Kate into the house. "Jesus, Kate! I was so worried. What's going on? Did you hear it? Did you see anything out there?" Kyle said while holding a trembling Kate in his arms. They squeezed each other for a solid minute.

"I was on the path in the woods when it started. I was terrified," Kate said, pulling away. "I have no idea what it was."

"Did you see anything exploding out there?" Kyle asked.

"No, just heard what sounded like rapid gunshots. They seemed to come from every direction." She walked into the living room and searched for the remote. Kate searched the couch cushions and the basket on the coffee table where it was supposed to live, but she and Kyle were both guilty of never returning it to its intended place. She also suspected Kyle hid it from her sometimes in an attempt to break her CNN pandemic death clock addiction. "Where's the damn remote, Kyle?"

"Hold on, hold on. I have it here." He rifled through the papers at his kitchen table desk. "I was trying to save you from the afternoon news." He turned on the TV.

"Reports are still coming in and our reporters on the ground are scrambling to make sense of what happened, but we can report what appears to be a series of mass shootings all over the city just moments ago. What's most confusing is these shots were fired at approximately the same time," a reporter explained in a voice that sounded like he was trying to convince himself.

A chill ran up her spine at the words "mass shooting," which would always remind Kate of Colorado and Theo Mast. A wave of nausea came over her so strong she put her hand over her mouth.

She flipped from the local news to cable; they too seemed confused.

"Just moments ago, there were multiple shootings in several cities. Our reporters are calling in from New York, Miami, Los Angeles, and here in Atlanta. Right now, all reporters are being told to take cover and stay safe. Everyone, Americans everywhere, should get inside a safe place and wait until law enforcement determines the cause and the culprits."

"Good advice," Kyle said to the TV. They both just stared at the screen.

After a few minutes listening to the reporters repeatedly advise people to seek shelter and stay inside, Kate walked to a window and peeked outside.

No cars or buses drove past their block, but she heard sirens off in the distance. They lived on a quiet side street with little traffic on a normal day and even less as a result of the pandemic. But right now, it seemed eerily calm. No people. No cars. Just trees swaying in the hot breeze.

A loud pop went off across the street. Kyle and Kate both jumped and quickly moved far from the window.

They looked around the house, like something might explode in their home. Then they looked at each other. Kate saw panic in Kyle's eyes for the first time in their relationship. Moving quietly, they slowly crept back to the window and peered out at the neighbor's house across the street.

At first, it looked quiet and normal.

"What the fuck is going on?" he whispered. "Why would someone target this neighborhood? No one important lives here."

"I don't know. But look. Does the window look weird or broken?" Kate whispered. "Maybe someone was shot? Part of the mass shooting? Or a home invasion?"

In a protective gesture, Kyle used his arm to back Kate away from the window.

In silence, Kate checked that the front door was locked, and Kyle ran to check the back. As he passed the kitchen, he grabbed his computer. Kyle drew the living room window curtains tightly closed, then they both ran upstairs to the bedroom which had only one small window. Kate closed the cheap miniblinds. She grabbed her personal laptop from the dresser, and they both sat on the bed and stared at their computers, switching from one news site to another. They also scrolled through Facebook and other social media.

"Let's check Twitter, too," Kate whispered, making Kyle jump.

Kate heard the confused barks of her next-door neighbor's dogs and was happy she and Kyle had found a forever home for Barny, an old pit mix they'd been fostering until a week ago. He wouldn't have liked the commotion. "They sound scared," Kate said to Kyle. "Did they just start barking?" She didn't recall hearing barking before. Not even in the woods. Were her ears tuned in to only explosions and scary noise or had everything really gone quiet?

"What?" Kyle asked, starting to scroll through Twitter. "Jesus Fucking Christ. They're now saying hundreds of simultaneous mass shootings were staged across the country. The entire country. All at the same time. Just after noon here, but also in Minneapolis, Portland, Chicago, Orlando, Billings, Austin, Charlotte... What the fuck? What the fuck, Kate? What the fuck?" Kyle almost never swore so Kate knew he was really upset.

They went downstairs and back to the TV. The news showed footage from cameras all over the country. Journalists reporting live at the time, security cameras, influencers doing Instagram live for their followers—footage all over with pops and explosions going off for a few minutes. There were zoom meeting recordings showing people ducking, running, screaming—and some people actually being shot.

"Preliminary reporting seems to indicate the shootings started in unison at 12:06 and ended around 12:15," an anchor reported. "People are finding dead bodies all over, in cars, in streets, in houses. It doesn't make any sense. This does not make any sense," she kept repeating.

"Shoot, maybe we should call the police about the neighbors with the broken window? They should check on them. See if they're okay." Kate said.

"That's a Black couple. Do you think calling the police is safe, Ms. Black Lives Matter?" Kyle responded in a not joking voice. He could not understand why Kate cared so much about racial justice and went to the protests and rallies. He supported the effort but did not think it was his, or Kate's, fight.

"Shut up," Kate said, dialing 911.

The busy signal squawked. The line was busy or she got an "all circuits are busy" recording every time she tried. "That's not comforting," Kate said. "We need to go over and make sure they're alright." Kate scrambled toward the door. She couldn't forgive herself if her neighbors were hurt, and they'd just sat there watching TV, doing nothing.

"Are you nuts?" Kyle asked, jumping up to block her way. "We are *not* leaving this house until we know what the hell happened. Seriously, Kate, don't be crazy. It could start again any minute. Where did the shooters go?"

Ugh. he had a good point. "Yes, I guess you're right," Kate agreed as she paced the small living room.

Staring at the TV for a few more minutes and repeatedly getting a busy tone or no tone for 911, Kate couldn't take the guilt. "But they might be hurt or bleeding to death or something. Stay here and watch me cross the street. I'll be so fast. I'll take a look and come right back," she told Kyle while unlocking the front door.

"Kate! No!" Kyle yelled, finally pulling his eyes away from Twitter.

She ran down the porch steps and bobbed and weaved across the street, up the neighbor's steps to their porch, creeping slow and quiet to the cracked window and peering in the hole, from which several large cracks fanned out in different directions.

She gasped. A body lay in front of the couch. Because of the angle, she couldn't see the head or face clearly. *Is that a shadow or a pool of blood?*

Kate's heart was beating so fast and loud she glanced down at her chest to see if she could actually see it. She then moved to the front door and knocked lightly. Her hand was shaking as she knocked again a little louder, afraid of who would answer.

"I'm nuts," Kate whispered to herself. "But they need help." She quietly tried the door knob. It was locked. She tried it again to be sure. She took a deep breath and whispered, "I'm sorry. I'll be back," and bobbed and weaved her way back to her house.

Kyle threw the door open and pulled her inside.

"I'm almost positive Yvette is laying on the floor, bleeding, maybe dead and shot!" Kate said in a gush.

"What the fuck!" Kyle said over and over, pacing the hall, his hands cupped over his head like he was preventing it from exploding. "Did you see the fucking shooter? I guess not or you would be fucking dead."

"Please stop swearing! Seriously, it's not helping!" Kate said, her annoyance with him making her voice go up an octave.

Kyle paced the foyer. "What should we do? We don't have a car. Lyft? Run? Stay?"

Kate had never seen him freak out like this before.

"You're talking about fleeing? Where to? Has the news changed? Are we still under attack?" Kate asked walking to the TV. Flipping stations, Kate found an anchor she trusted. "Let's see what Bianca is telling us to do."

"Maybe we should move back upstairs, away from all these windows?" Kyle suggested.

But Kate was not listening to him.

"According to updated reports coming in from local officials and reporters in multiple cities, what happened today, which we are still trying to make sense of, was not some coordinated mass shooting. A mass shooting, by definition, has multiple victims, from one or two shooters. For example, one person shooting family members, or several people at a church service, or school, or some social gathering like a concert or movie. What happened today is unprecedented. Viewers, if you have small children in the room, you may want to cover their ears for what we are about to report."

Kate and Kyle looked at each other. She saw her own fear reflected in his eyes. She pushed back memories of Colorado; she didn't have time to slide down another rabbit hole of stress. She'd think about it later.

"This new fact we have ascertained makes what happened today seem even more unfathomable, but there are dead and wounded police officers all over the country. We are getting reports from everywhere—cities, suburbs, rural counties in every state. It would seem that in addition to thousands of Americans, cops were definitely targeted," Bianca said with tears in her eyes.

"Jesus fucking mother of God Christ," Kyle yelled, tugging at his hair. "Shooters, murderers everywhere, and we are down hundreds of cops!"

Kate thought about the Sheriff in Colorado who was going to take care of everything. She thought of the President's Blue Lives Matter followers and their idolization of cops, as long as the cops did their bidding. Was this some sort of twisted revenge attack? The President's supporters were inclined to celebrate violence. Hell, the President publicly celebrated and encouraged violence. She just hoped that whatever, whoever it was, it didn't make it harder for the Black Lives Matter movement.

"Who the fuck shoots hundreds of cops?" Kyle asked as Kate rubbed his back.

"I don't know, baby. It's all so horrible," Kate added with tears in her eyes.

THREE

The Day of the Shooting

As the hours went by, Kate and Kyle just stared at the TV, flipping around between local and national news. When Kate realized she was shivering, she went upstairs to change out of her running clothes, still damp with sweat from her earlier run.

She occasionally peeked out the window and looked across the street.

"Pick up for Christ's sake," she yelled at her cell as she continued to try to get 911 to answer. "All circuits are still busy," she mumbled. "This is unacceptable!" She felt horrible thinking about Yvette and equally horrible thinking of dead police officers.

Just after 7:00 p.m., the anchors seemed to have pulled more information together. They were interviewing firefighters and EMT ambulance service providers who had been in homes and businesses trying to help gunshot victims.

"First responders report they are getting hundreds of calls and have asked the public to be patient; they will get to you as soon as possible," Bianca told the camera before cutting away to a live interview.

"I would say we are seeing a pattern here," a red-eyed New York City police officer said to the microphones thrust in his face as he tried to enter an apartment building in Hell's Kitchen.

"What pattern?" yelled a particularly loud and aggressive reporter. Maybe he yelled because of his mask. It was New York, so everyone was wearing masks.

The police officer paused to collect his thoughts. "I've been to the scene of four shootings since approximately 12:15 today. That includes a police station on 33rd. I've seen dozens of dead bodies. It appears upon initial review, and this could change, that these people shot themselves with their own firearms. These may not be mass shootings as we have previously understood mass shootings but may be mass suicides. We will let you know more as we continue our investigations." He turned and walked away from the reporters.

A feeling of dread spread through Kate's stomach. She remembered a large bag, with who knows how many guns, and the terror of not knowing what Theo Mast intended to do. *Murder? Suicide?*

"No way you are leaving," said the big, loud reporter blocking the cop's exit. He seemed like he was seven feet tall and towered over the police officer. "People are terrified. There is a big difference between mass shootings and mass suicides. Do you really think all these people shot themselves? What about the police? Who shot them?" He continued so loudly that the cop could not ignore the important questions.

Bile rose in her throat.

"Look, the first two calls today were individuals in their homes. Did someone break in? Did a friend or family member shoot them and leave? The situations did not fit the typical profile for home invasions. Was it someone they knew? But the..." he gulped, "the position of the gunshot wounds seem self-inflicted"

"What the hell," Kyle said, staring at the screen, squeezing Kate's hand so hard she thought he might bruise her.

Reporters shouted more questions to the cop, and he yelled back, "We have to wait for the coroner's reports. I'm just offering this information now to potentially calm some people. Though I am not sure this helps family members. I mean, isn't it better that we don't have assailants running around shooting people, right?" He sighed deeply and continued. "At the police station, where almost everyone was armed, it appears that the individuals shot themselves. How could a shooter, or even multiple shooters, get so close to trained and armed police officers? Someone there, of all places, would have shot the shooter," he said, almost as a question to himself.

The gaggle of reporters continued their tirade, shouting questions and raising hands like they were in grade school hoping to be picked next.

"Look, I've said enough for now. We need more facts. I'm just remarking on a trend we're starting to see." He finished and walked quickly away, leaving the reporters stunned to silence while processing his words.

"Did he just say he thinks the cops shot themselves?" A reporter asked another reporter while still on a hot mike.

They cut away from Hell's Kitchen, and the network anchors suddenly appeared. Faces grim, one of them took an audible breath. "We'll take a quick break and try to corroborate what the police officer said."

"No wonder we can't get through to 911 or get anyone to check on Yvette," Kate said to Kyle.

"That was in New York. We don't know if that happened here. Why would it?" Kyle said, watching a commercial on TV.

"Why wouldn't it?" Kate responded. "I mean, that would explain the '*all circuits are busy*' for seven hours. Cops will look after and investigate their own situations first. Especially involving shootings at police stations. I mean, they will look after their own first—it's only natural."

Kyle rolled his eyes, which he only did when super annoyed; he didn't like her immediate suspicion of the police. "They will come as soon as they can," he said.

Kate and Kyle watched news coverage late into the night. At one point, they took a break and nuked canned soup. Kyle downed a couple of beers, but Kate couldn't stomach even one.

PTSD, Kate thought, watching her hands shake.

By 2:00 a.m., the news anchors were sure of one thing: millions of Americans had been shot in every state and every city, from sea to shining sea, and in Alaska and Hawaii. Just as unfathomable, it seemed there were countless deaths across the globe. The scope of the horror was starting to sink in. No place was spared. Mass shootings at approximately the same time, everywhere.

FOUR

The Day After the Shooting

Kate snapped awake in the wee hours of the morning, jolted by a terrible nightmare. She had fallen asleep on the couch. As she blinked her eyes open, she lost the details of the dream but had a cold, hard feeling in her stomach. Just like so many mornings since the unstable liar was sworn in as President.

This is normal; of course, I'm stressed. The pandemic is killing tens of thousands, the planet is dying, the worldwide economy is collapsing, the Administration is hurting and destroying everything I love. An anxiety attack is perfectly normal.

"Kyle!" she shouted.

He jerked awake. "What? What? Are you okay, babe?"

"Was there really a nation-wide mass shooting yesterday?" she asked.

Kyle sat up and looked at the muted TV. He clicked the volume up.

"Yes. A mass shooting, everywhere at once, remember? Millions are dead. Millions of Americans are dead. Or wait, not a mass shooting, a mass suicide," Kyle said slowly as if he was reminding himself.

As their minds fully woke, the news anchor's words started to make sense.

"I hoped it was a nightmare," Kate said, turning the volume up.

"What we now know for sure is that the shootings were not just in America but across the planet. All at approximately the same time or within a fifteen-minute window. Hundreds of millions of people are dead. Millions of police officers and soldiers are dead. We have a representative from Homeland Security joining us to discuss why this happened."

A man introduced as a senior policy advisor appeared on the screen. He looked like a deer in headlights. He had deep circles under his eyes. "I need to be clear right away: we have no idea why this happened. None. Why would millions of people commit suicide at the same time? We are looking into some kind of a cyberattack. Or perhaps a mass drugging? We have considered and rejected an attack from a foreign nation or sect because the incident happened in every country. The usual suspects, Russia, China, Iran, North Korea, all seem to be reeling from this tragedy. In fact, many heads of state are dead. Just like many in leadership at Homeland Security." The man seemed to get more distressed as he spoke.

Was the Secretary of Homeland Security dead? Kate felt a chill run through her body. *Are any of my Space Force colleagues dead? My old colleagues from NASA? Is our government even functioning?*

"Who's in charge?" Kyle asked, and Kate just shook her head.

"We are so sorry for your loss. Are you saying the Administration has no idea what caused this crisis?" asked the anchor.

"Yes, that is correct," the senior policy advisor replied.

"What should Americans be doing now, today, as they wake-up and realize the full extent of what happened?" the anchor asked.

"As head of logistics at Homeland, I can tell you that I know people are scared, but they need to remain calm and focused. I understand that many Americans have dead bodies, dead loved ones, in their homes."

Kate thought of Yvette. *Is she still on the floor? Did her husband come home to find her there?*

"Many victims did not die from their gunshot wounds, so our hospitals, already stressed with COVID, are busy. We also know many people are dead, so we're asking all refrigeration truck owners from all industries to call their local officials to make arrangements for their trucks to be used for body storage. That will help make space in the hospitals for the living. We need to help people remove the deceased and get them stored safely. If people have not been directly impacted, please help your neighbors, family, and friends. Stay out of hospitals and away from doctors, so they can focus on the living victims. If you can give blood, call your local blood bank and donate. It's been 18 hours, and I know people are in shock. They are tired, and many are mourning, but we all need to work together to save American lives." The official sounded exhausted and a little incoherent.

"See, we were right to check on Yvette," Kate said, nudging Kyle and feeling sick thinking of her still lying there.

The agent continued. "We also need to understand that no one else has been shot since yesterday, so the threat seems to have passed. Please stay inside your home or a safe location. We don't know why it happened or if it will happen again. For right now, it's only safe to go outside if you need to help others. Only go out if you are helping yourself or others in a medical emergency. And of course, wear a mask and keep social distancing. We are still in a pandemic."

"Wow. That is a lot to process but very, very helpful," the anchor said, shaking her head. "Now we will let you get back to work, your very important work."

"Thank you. Be safe, fellow Americans," the government official said before disappearing from the screen.

I wonder if this guy's a career employee, like me, or a political hack appointed because he made a big donation to the campaign. It's hard to trust anyone in this administration. It's always good to question authority, even if only to oneself.

"Well, viewers, you heard him, directly from Homeland Security. If you have a wounded person in the home, take them to the hospital. If you have a victim in your home, hold on; a system is being set up to help with the deceased. It's okay and helpful to check on your neighbors and make a blood donation, but otherwise, stay home." She repeated what the government official said in a more coherent way.

"We need to give blood," Kate and Kyle said at almost the exact time while staring at the TV.

Kate laughed but then felt immediately bad for doing so.

"This whole thing fucking sucks," Kyle said. "Jesus. First COVID and now this. It's incomprehensible. Why is this shit happening?"

Kate felt crazy stress energy surging through her veins. Under normal circumstances, she'd head to the trail for a run. Instead, she showered, dried her hair, and dressed in 20 minutes flat. "I'm so anxious. I feel like a hurricane is coming, or something terrible is imminent and we need to be ready."

"It's PTSD. It's just too much. Our systems are in overdrive," Kyle said, pulling her in for a hug.

While Kyle showered, Kate prepared breakfast. She put cereal, fruit, oat milk, and coffee on the table and decided to make vegetarian sausage. "We need to eat hearty if we are giving blood," Kate said to Kyle as he walked into the kitchen.

"Right. Good thinking," he said, sitting down. "First we should check on our neighbors to make sure everyone is okay."

As Kate was shoving a spoon of cereal in her mouth, she paused. She didn't feel hungry, but she needed food to avoid fainting while she gave blood. "It's only six-thirty? Maybe we should wait until eight?"

"I doubt people are sleeping in, but yeah, let's wait until eight," Kyle agreed.

"Wonder if the blood bank is doing normal hours?" Kate asked.

They ate in silence for a few minutes. The idea of sitting around, waiting an hour to do something seemed impossible. It was so quiet that they both jumped when the AC kicked on.

"I can't take it. Let's go out and see what the hell is happening," Kyle said, standing up.

"I'll grab masks," Kate said.

FIVE

The Day After the Shooting

K ate and Kyle walked across the street. The sun
was up, and it was totally quiet: no people, cars,
honking, or sirens. There wasn't even a bird chirping
or dog barking.

"It's too quiet," Kate whispered.

They walked up to the front and looked through
Yvette's window. Nothing seemed to have changed
since Kate peeked in the day before.

"Damn, is that her?" Kyle whispered with his face
against the glass. "It's so dark in there."

This time Kate knocked loudly and yelled, "Yvette?"
She tried the handle. "The door is still locked. Let's
check windows. See if we can get in." They started to
walk around to the back of the house.

"We might have to pull a screen and just break one,"
Kyle suggested as they walked.

They snaked around to the back alley and located
Yvette's row house behind a very tall fence. Kyle shook
the fence door hard. The lock slipped, and they rushed
through the small back yard and up the steps to the

back door. When they got to the back door, they both jumped as they heard a male voice in the house crying, "Oh God, oh God, no!"

They ran back around to the front and saw the front door now wide open. Sticking their heads in, they saw Sinclair, Yvette's husband, on the ground cradling her body.

The way he held her, it was clear she was dead.

Kate backed out and pulled Kyle with her. "Let's give him a minute."

They could hear him speaking low to her and sniffling loudly. He suddenly jumped up and reached for his phone.

Kate heard the familiar tones and "All circuits are busy." Sinclair was trying to call 911.

"Sinclair? Hey it's Kate and Kyle from across the street. Can we help?"

Sinclair flinched when Kate spoke.

She walked closer to him but kept her distance since he was not wearing a mask. "We've been trying to call 911 since yesterday. I think they're overwhelmed. Should we drive her to the hospital? We can drive..." Kate offered. She knew Sinclair had a car.

"Is she dead?" Kyle asked quietly.

"Yes," Sinclair said, his voice quivering. "I wish I had been here." He hugged Yvette's body tightly.

"Homeland Security said to keep the dead at home. They're creating a system to collect people. The hospitals are too busy," Kyle added in a kind voice.

They all stayed silent as Sinclair hugged and rocked Yvette.

"Screw that," Sinclair said suddenly, standing and scooping up Yvette's body.

Kate and Kyle lunged forward to help. Yvette was a small, fit woman, but she was dead weight. There was dried blood everywhere. Kate couldn't tell where the bullet had gone through Yvette and into the front window.

Together, they were able to get Yvette into the backseat of Sinclair's car. Sinclair sat with her, and Kate and Kyle climbed in the front.

"Wait," Kate said. "Maybe I should stay. Check in on the rest of the neighbors. Others may need help as well."

Kate pulled her mask away briefly and mouthed the words "help him" to Kyle, and he nodded back. Kate got out of the car.

She looked at Sinclair with tears in her eyes. There were no correct words as he cradled his dead wife's body in the backseat of his car.

Kate watched the car drive away.

She walked slowly down the street, checking her watch and seeing it was just after seven. Time was moving so slowly. Kate was hesitant to knock on doors. All seemed so quiet on what was otherwise another muggy D.C. morning.

She kept seeing Yvette's lifeless body. Her hands started to shake as tears slid down her cheeks.

Being productive and helpful usually feels good, Kate thought, but now she felt horrible. As she continued to walk down the street, swallowing hard and trying to breathe, she noticed that lights were on in windows. They were mostly upstairs windows. She could see the glow of big flat screen TVs and realized people were up, just staring at screens like she and Kyle had been.

She decided to just go for it and knock on doors.

Kate spoke to many of her neighbors on both sides of the streets. Most were like her and Kyle, shocked and addicted to the news. People repeated what was said on the news or what they saw on social media, but no one was speculating to the cause.

Because of the pandemic lockdown, almost all the neighbors were home. Few came out of their homes to speak with Kate; they just stuck their heads out the doors to talk. A new terrifying mix of fear was present: COVID and the shootings. Kate told only the closest neighbors what happened to Yvette and how Sinclair and Kyle were at the hospital.

When she had checked in on everyone on the street, she started making phone calls to her parents, siblings, friends, and colleagues. She and Kyle had already texted most people and shared that they were safe on social media, but she wanted to hear voices. Calls were finally going through again.

She led with this on every call:

"Hi. I know it's not a good time; we are all in shock. I just wanted to hear your voice and make sure you are alright," she repeated for hours.

Of course, she FaceTimed with her mom the longest.

"Kate, I am so happy you and Kyle are okay! I haven't left my condo since it happened. There were so many gunshots in every direction. I hit the ground because I could hear them through the walls. I thought whoever was shooting up the other condos would be coming after me. It's a miracle no bullets came through the walls, literally a miracle. Now they say it was people shooting themselves with their own guns? Many of my students' parents have guns. I weep for what they saw. I bet I lost students. What on Earth caused people to shoot themselves?"

Kate just let her mother rant and talk for some time. When she paused, Kate jumped in. "I have never been so terrified for you living in Florida. Not when a hurricane had your city in the bullseye, not when your governor refused a mask mandate, but this is it. You are leaving Florida. That state is too deadly."

"Well, let's just get through this and then decide what's next," her mom replied. "And it's been so quiet since yesterday. Not a single airplane. Reminds me of the days after 9-11. Of course, you were too young to remember that nightmare. Well, the first few days of the pandemic lockdown also had this terrifying silence."

"All I remember about 9-11 was you staring at the TV 24/7 and eating pizza take-out for days," Kate said.

"And I'm sure this is on your mind too, darling. The shooting makes me think of Colorado," her mom said.

"Me too, Mom," Kate said, feeling like she'd been kicked in the gut. "Me too. God, I hate guns."

"My neighbor is at the door. Let me see what she needs. I'll call you later. I love you so much," her mom said before hanging up.

Kate didn't frequently let herself think about Colorado, a defense mechanism she employed to keep herself sane. But since the shootings started, images and memories kept skirting the edges of her mind.

To hear her mother acknowledge it too made her break down and sob.

She jumped when, hours later, Kyle came through the front door, looking very pale.

"It's crazy out there. The hospital was overflowing, and most of the patients are dead. The emergency room, where Sinclair and I waited for three hours, is full of people holding their dead loved ones. Staff would come by and ask lots of questions. Lots of forms. Lots of paperwork. Lots of confusion. Doctors would eventually come by and declare the patient dead and put that in a computer. I had planned to stay with Sinclair until they took Yvette's body, but his friend arrived. Yvette's mom was trying to come to D.C. despite Sinclair repeatedly telling her travel was not safe. I guess she lives in Detroit. Anyway, I thought it was okay to leave," Kyle said slowly. "I've been crying all morning. You would have lost it completely, babe. So much blood. So much sadness and pain and trauma." He plopped down on the couch and looked at the TV. Then he added, "TVs are on everywhere. Still don't seem to know what caused the shooting or mass suicide. It's so sad."

Kate moved closer to him and massaged his shoulders. He leaned his head against her. She felt the weight of his sadness.

"What's going on here?" He turned to look at her. "Did you talk to the neighbors?"

"Checked in on everyone. Yvette seems to be the only victim on our street. Of course, the Ennis family is still in Wisconsin, so I'm not sure how they are. Everyone is just freaked out. Some of their friends and family were victims. Not everyone is accounted for yet. But some good news: I spoke to most of my family and some of yours, and there are no direct victims. I heard some tragic stories. Seriously Kyle, it's crazy, but I think we were spared the worst."

Kyle reached for her, pulling her down on to the couch with him. They held each other for several minutes, both crying softly.

SIX

The Day After the Shooting

"**I** can't believe it's only 2 p.m.," Kate said. "It's been like what, twenty-four hours? I guess twenty-six to be exact. Feels like days." She stared at the TV, watching images of police stations full of bodies. Prison and jails were in chaos because so many guards had shot themselves. The military had been hit hard too. "This reminds me of 9-11, watching my mom stare at the TV for 24 hours straight. How many dead bodies have we seen on TV today?"

"I saw too many in real life at the hospital," Kyle replied. "And we both saw Yvette's," he added.

"I have no idea how healthcare workers are holding it together. The pandemic and now this? How can we help?" Kate asked.

She started making calls. The hospital was just a couple of miles away, and there were many pizza places, coffee shops, and other food joints between here and there doing take-out during the pandemic. If any restaurants were open today, she would send food and coffee to the hospital. This endeavor kept her busy for a while, and then she remembered giving blood.

"Kyle, we forgot to go give blood!" she said, excited to have another productive thing to do.

"Ugh, I wish we could, but there was a line down the street at the hospital blood bank. The hospital is in chaos. We would be in the way."

Kate paced around the living room. She picked up the remote and switched the channel. "Let's check in on local news. See what they say. Maybe they have recommendations on what specific help is needed here."

The local anchor read slowly from the teleprompter. "We now know that the incident was not isolated to law enforcement and military. Anyone with a gun in their possession shot themselves around noon yesterday with the vast majority of those shootings being fatal."

"Holy shit," Kate's hand flew over her mouth. Anyone with a gun. Her mind flashed back to the weapons in Theo's duffle bag.

Had he killed himself?

"We previously reported that the shootings took place between 12:06 pm and 12:15 p.m.; however, it seems the shootings occurred during an estimated fifteen-minute window, ending at 12:21. We are reporting the facts about our beloved city as they come in. There are almost 60,000 registered guns in D.C. and thousands more that are not registered. People that own guns tend to own more than one. Until recently, the district had some of the strictest gun laws in the country, and personal gun ownership is still very low compared to other cities. However, we have a large percentage of armed law enforcement, including the

D.C. police force, Secret Service, Capitol Hill police, and other federal agents. Just moments ago, the mayor commented that if the correlation between gun owner-ship and the shootings is consistent across the country, one hundred million Americans may have shot them-selves yesterday."

Kate and Kyle looked at each other. "One hundred million? Is that what she said?" Kate asked.

Kyle gulped and nodded his head. "Like a third of our entire population."

"Local hospitals and morgues in the district are overwhelmed," the reporter continued. "The mayor has set up hotlines for residents to call and report the need to claim and store a body."

The news station showed live footage of refrigera-tion trucks rolling into D.C. What looked like dozens at first, then hundreds, rolled down 66 and I-95 like a somber parade. The trucks had all kinds of logos: gro-cery stores, beer distributors, meat packing plants—anything that could store bodies while the chaos was being sorted out.

"If truck drivers were not considered frontline heroes before, they sure are now. Collecting hundreds of bodies is certainly going above and beyond," Kyle said, staring at the TV.

"So all gun owners around the world just took them out of their holster or closet or from under their bed and shot themselves?" Kate questioned out loud. "Or maybe they had them locked up in a gun safe box or fancy gun cabinet. So they got out a key, unlocked the lock, took out the gun, and pointed it at their own head or throat or mouth or heart. And maybe, around noon, after they took the gun out of whatever or wherever they kept it, they looked into it, and realized it did not have bullets. Then they located the bullets and loaded the gun. Maybe that took a few minutes. Then they put the gun to a part of their body and squeezed the trigger. Maybe that..." Kate continued, staring at the screen at the caravan of refrigeration trucks rolling down the highway toward the city.

"Jesus, Kate. Yes, probably. Sounds like that's what they think happened. That's what the mayor said earlier," Kyle said, cutting her off and sounding more stressed due to Kate's graphic musings.

"I'm trying to figure out the timeline. Maybe it took people time to find their guns, and maybe it took more time to find the bullets and load it. Maybe some people could not find the gun or bullets right away? Maybe they had to clean the gun? Do guns need to be cleaned before they shoot? Seems like people in the movies have to clean their guns. Maybe that takes time?" Kate wondered.

"I don't know. I haven't seen a gun in years. I went to a shooting range a couple of times in college, but it was not my gun; it was handed to me loaded with bullets. I have no idea if they need to be cleaned," Kyle said.

"But why fifteen minutes?" Kate asked.

"What?" Kyle asked.

"The media reported the timeline wrong at first. A shorter window. Was it in the paper? Did the anchor just say fifteen? It sure seemed longer than fifteen minutes to me. The shooting started at around noon and lasted fifteen minutes? Maybe longer? Like Yvette? We heard that at like 12:20, right?" Kate asked.

"Yes. I guess. Seems right. What are you thinking?" Kyle said, now staring at Kate.

"I'm just wondering if the people who took longer were trying not to shoot themselves. Maybe they tried to stop themselves? Questioned the decision? What was the reason? Why would they shoot themselves at all?" Kate's mind was rapid fire trying to make sense of the incident.

"Terminators," Kyle said it like a fact, not a joke.

Kate rolled her eyes. Kyle was obsessed with those movies. He often recited lines from them.

"Seriously, think about it, Kate. Maybe the guns came alive somehow," Kyle went on.

"That's stupid. Guns don't have chips. They aren't attached to apps," Kate said, looking at the TV.

"Maybe they are," Kyle said, scoffing at Kate's sound logic. "You don't know. You've never even touched a gun. Maybe they're high-tech now. We just don't know."

"Wait, why would they have chips or apps? If they did, the guns, and maybe the bullets, could be tracked more easily. They wouldn't have to wait for forensics to analyze bullets after a murder, police shooting, or poaching incident. They could just check the app to know whose gun it was and maybe why it went off." Kate was excited at the idea. "That would actually be very cool." She smiled at Kyle.

"But then the terminators could control them," Kyle said seriously. Suddenly, he started to laugh. "You're crazy and have no idea what you are talking about!"

"Me?" Kate laughed. "I'm crazy?"

Kyle got up suddenly and picked Kate up off the couch, cradling her in his arms.

"Stop!" Kate squealed as he scooped her up.

"I still think it's safer upstairs," he said as he bounded up the stairs, still holding Kate.

Kate was laughing and yelling to put her down, but she did not mean it. She loved that Kyle was so strong and could easily carry her. It really turned her on.

Kyle could be annoying sometimes, more conservative than Kate liked, but he was one of the most attractive men she had ever seen. When she met him volunteering at a community cleanup event, he took her breath away. She could not stop staring at him. He was taller than she was but not too tall, just under 6 feet. He was muscular and wore an old college t-shirt that was tight across the shoulders and chest. His forearms were tan and drove Kate crazy; it made it very hard for her to focus on picking up litter. And he had stunning blue eyes.

She was more aggressive than she had ever been with a man before and followed him along a path, picking up plastic bottles, beer cans, and fast-food wrappings until he finally spoke to her. They chatted and laughed and picked up trash for hours, well passed the official time to turn in the garbage bags. They went out to get lunch and beers after and basically never stopped talking.

"We can't do this while the world is falling apart," Kate said, still giggling as Kyle put her down on the bed and kissed her lips, cheeks, and neck. "This is really inappropriate," Kate continued, but Kyle just kept kissing her.

SEVEN

Twenty-Nine Hours After the Shooting

K ate was laying naked across the bed. It was hot outside, so even with the AC on, it was stuffy and warm in the small bedroom. Kyle was dozing off. They had spent the past couple of hours making love.

Kyle is fantastic in bed, Kate thought while rubbing his light brown hair. He kind of looked like a frat boy from an 80's movie or someone that played lacrosse in college.

For those two hours of intense sex, she forgot about the shootings, the pandemic, all the death, and people mourning enormous loss. As reality came rushing back, her heart started to race, and her breathing became noticeable.

"Kyle, wake-up!" she snapped.

Kyle jerked awake and sat up. "What's wrong?" he demanded. He looked her up and down and immediately realized she was fine—and still naked. "What's wrong, baby? Nightmare? I guess daymare?" he asked. "What time is it?" Kyle leaned over to kiss Kate.

After a long, slow kiss, she broke away and sat up. "I just had this intense wave of guilt. We were joking around. We're having day sex. Wait, work day sex, while millions of people are in physical pain and hundreds of millions in emotional trauma. I feel terrible," Kate stated sadly. Tears started to pour from her eyes. "I haven't even checked in with work. Neither of us have."

What if on top of all this, we both lost our jobs? In this economy, we'll be screwed.

Kate did not enjoy her job. She spent a lot of time trying to persuade political appointees that taking money away from Space Force was not okay. They claimed defense along the Mexico border was the same thing as defense of space, insisting Congress wanted Americans safe.

"The President would rather the money was spent on his frigging wall. I promise you that," one very young, persistent appointee would often call to say.

Maybe it would not be so bad to lose my job. I'm tired of explaining how appropriations work. If the President wanted funds for Space Force, and he got Congress to designate it to Space Force, it should go to Space Force. I mean, Americans should be equally afraid of immigrants as aliens. They are as equally dangerous and deserve the same defense funding— which should be zero dollars. I would love to tell these idiots to spend the money on solar panels and wind turbines because we really need protection from climate change.

"It's after six. We're no longer at work," Kyle said with a sigh. "Plus, everyone was doing what we were doing today."

Kate seriously doubted it, but she hoped he was right.

"I feel sad for the losses but not bad we had sex," Kyle added, a little defensively. Clearly, he thought one had nothing to do with the other. "We don't own guns. So far, except for Yvette, which is heartbreaking, we don't know anyone that died in the shooting. Though I bet that will change as people are identified. Like my college friends, some must own guns? And what about your friends in Florida?" Kyle kept talking. "Do we know any police? People in the military? How do we not know cops and active-duty soldiers? We are at war," Kyle continued, thinking out loud. "Anyway, what is the saying? *Live by the gun, die by the gun?* Who said that? Ronald Regan? In a movie? Or is it *violence begets violence?*"

"I think the origin of the idea is '*Live by the sword, die by the sword*' from the Bible," Kate responded, even though she'd barely been to church in her life.

"Oh right. That makes sense," Kyle said, laying back on the bed, still naked.

"Ronald Regan?" Kate said rolling her eyes again as she pulled her previously discarded t-shirt over her head.

"I think he said that in a movie," Kyle added, sounding defensive again.

"I wouldn't know," Kate said, getting up and heading to the bathroom.

"Wait, didn't he say *'I will keep shooting people until they take my gun out of my cold, dead hands'*?" Kate asked.

"I don't think that was Reagan. Why would he say that? He was shot, remember?" Kyle asked incredulously.

"I don't know. Someone famous said something like that. Look it up," Kate added. "I am going to take a shower. Then maybe take a walk and see if we can help or do something productive."

If the chaos of yesterday was self-inflicted, then fears of being outside are pointless.

EIGHT

Thirty Hours After the Shooting

Kate walked for a half hour in her neighborhood and on the wooded trails, but aside from getting some exercise, she had accomplished nothing. Everyone seemed locked in their homes, terrified. She returned home and sat on the couch, frustrated with her helpless impotence.

She flipped channels, anxious again. The news just kept showing bodies being carried into hospitals, crazy emergency room scenes, and refrigeration trucks all across America. The footage from other countries was just as bad. In some developing countries, people were digging mass graves. They didn't have thousands of refrigeration options available; they had to bury their dead quickly before they caused additional public health disasters. The anchors and reporters were not even bothering to say, "Warning, this footage contains graphic images," anymore because there were dead bodies, dead people, everywhere.

Tears rolled down Kate's face as she stared at the screen. "Jesus Christ," she said loudly, just as Kyle walked down the stairs.

"Let's nuke a meal. I'm starved," Kyle said, turning off the TV. "It's not helping to watch this over and over. We know what happened. Or at least as much as anyone knows now. Let's eat and then take a walk," he said, heading to the kitchen.

"I just took a walk. It didn't help," Kate said.

As Kate ate her organic vegan frozen meal, she had a thought. "What about the NRA? They haven't made any statement yet, right? How are they defending this?" Kate said, reaching for her phone. She did a quick news search, then looked at the gun lobby's social media. "Nope, nothing. Not a peep. Not even on Twitter. What is their game? Stay quiet until the dust settles? Global thoughts and prayers?"

"I hate the NRA as much as you, but they're probably all dead. I bet anyone that works for the NRA owns at least one gun. Most probably own several. All kinds too: automatic weapons, rifles, handguns, all kinds. They probably have open carry policy at work. I bet their offices are a mess right now," Kyle continued.

Kate was quiet for a full minute thinking about it.

"Oh my God, you're right. That's sad. So many lives lost. What about their kids? So many orphans. Kids don't own guns," Kate said, eyes welling up again. *Not little kids.* "Well, I bet some NRA little ones do own guns. It's so, so sad." She wiped away the tears rolling down her cheeks.

Kyle reached for her hand, still wet from the tears. "Hey. We can't help what happened. It's sad to think about so many senseless deaths. Not just this, but the pandemic. These last six months have been a cluster fuck nightmare. And it's getting worse." He stroked her palm.

"Has there been a mass shooting since the pandemic started? I know there have been shootings, but no mass shootings, right? I guess we all know what the parents and loved ones in Columbine, Sandy Hook, Orlando, Vegas feel like, not to mention synagogues, churches, movie theaters, Wal-Mart, etc. etc. etc. feel." Kate's voice petered out, overwhelmed by the list. "The things we just start to accept as normal. I guess we're all survivors of a mass shooting now. The whole country. The whole world," Kate continued, tears flowing down her face.

"Live by the gun, die by the gun," Kyle mumbled, kissing her hand, then releasing it to pick up their dishes. "Come on. Let's get out of here," he said.

Kate wiped her cheeks and blew her nose, pulling herself together. "Yes, I need to get out of here," Kate said. "I feel claustrophobic."

As they walked through the neighborhood and headed downtown, they stopped to ask people if they were okay or needed anything. Most folks seemed startled and moved quickly away. Amid the pandemic, people found it unnecessary to speak to strangers, even with masks. Of course, now the global shooting had everyone on edge.

"We really don't know what caused it, so maybe it could happen again." Kate said to Kyle.

"Aren't all the gun owners dead or injured though?" he said, draping an arm over her shoulder.

As they got closer to downtown and the hospital, more people were gathered in the streets and on the sidewalks. Most wore masks and social distanced. Except for ambulances and refrigeration trucks, there were few vehicles. Kate almost missed the normalcy of pre-pandemic bumper to bumper traffic.

It was almost nine o'clock; the sky was growing dark.

Kate heard a few people arguing loudly. As they got closer, she could make out the words.

"God fucking did this!" one man, wearing a mask around his chin, shouted at another.

"Why would God kill millions of people? You're a major fucking asshole," shouted the other man.

"He did it before with a flood; this time he did it with guns!" the first man shouted back. "Guns are faster. He could kill more with guns than floods!"

"Why would He do that?" demanded the second man.

A woman sitting on a bench nearby stood-up and yelled to be heard through her mask, "Because we are corrupt and filled with violence! You don't know your Bible!"

Kate looked at Kyle. "Live by the sword, die by the sword," Kate whispered as they walked by.

"Wow, people are really tense," Kyle said to Kate as they quickly walked to the hospital emergency entrance. "Between the pandemic and the shooting, it does seem biblical. Like end of days," Kyle added.

They walked to the emergency room sliding doors and decided not to go in. They could hear crying and see chaos and knew they could not help. Then they walked to the main hospital entrance and saw dozens of pizza boxes and coffee containers stacked on the information counter. Kyle walked over to a staff person and asked if they needed anything. The receptionist offered Kyle pizza.

Kate waited near the door, watching.

When he walked back to Kate, he said, "Many good Samaritans had your same idea. That woman said they don't need anything we can provide."

"I feel totally useless," Kate said as they walked toward home.

"2020 sucks so bad," Kyle replied.

Kate started to cry. Kyle paused and pulled her into a tight, long hug.

"I think we need sleep," Kyle whispered in her ear. "Things will be better tomorrow."

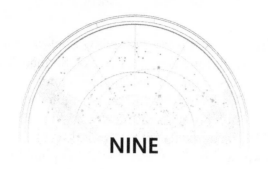

NINE

Two Days After the Shooting

I n the morning, Kate checked into work for the first time since the shooting to read emails and Slack messages. Her supervisor and colleagues had also started to communicate and check in. Her immediate supervisor lost both her son and father and was taking time off. They had confirmation that two people in her division had shot themselves and were dead.

The official word from the top of Space Force and Office of Personnel Management was that all non-essential staff had the rest of the week off to deal with the fallout from the shooting.

There were additional words, including "thoughts and prayers" going out to all impacted staff.

Kate almost dreaded having the rest of the week off, even if it was just two more days. It was like the first few months of the pandemic all over again. What to do to fill the anxious sad hours?

As she ate breakfast, Kyle walked into the kitchen.

"I don't work until Monday," Kyle said.

Kate just nodded.

"But I bet it's passed Monday. I bet we don't go back to work for a couple of weeks. So many people have lost loved ones. Plus, I'm sure many companies have to figure out who will do what jobs now. Think about it, millions of people are dead. Who will do their jobs? It's incomprehensible," he continued.

"I know. This is worse than the beginning of the pandemic. At least we had work to distract us," Kate said, finishing her breakfast.

"I wonder how many farmers and grocery store clerks own guns? Truck drivers and factory workers? Will this disrupt the food chain like when the workers in slaughterhouses got COVID? The pandemic didn't impact food supply much, but maybe this will?" Kate worried. "Maybe that's how we can help—go work on a farm or in a grocery store? At least until we have to go back to work."

"Okay, babe," Kyle said, patting her head. "You get your overalls on and start planting."

"I'm serious! We might not feel the strain right away, but there are going to be food shortages for sure. Course, I wouldn't mind if the meat industry shut down. I think it's time for a vegan revolution. That would also reduce the chances of another pandemic," Kate added while sipping coffee. "Maybe something good could come from this nightmare."

"And there's a third less Americans to feed," Kyle said. "There may be less of a food shortage than you think, Kate."

As Kate walked into the living room, the news caught her attention. CNN was interviewing a commander at a military installation. "Soldiers that live on base don't directly own their guns, so there were fewer dead than expected. However, many soldiers that live off base own personal guns. They still don't know how many have died. We'd like to reassure Americans that the U.S. is being defended," he said, staring into the camera with steely gray eyes and a square jaw. Kate was surprised this guy didn't own a gun. "And since other nations, including Iraq, Iran, North Korea, and Russia, are struggling with their own mass shooting deaths, this is not a military oriented national security crisis at this point. The military is getting engaged only to help Americans."

"Yeah, right," Kate said as she rolled her eyes. Her distrust of authority included the Department of Defense, its leadership anyway.

He continued, "Similar to the aftermath of a natural disaster, we are here for America, and we will pull together and rise up." Kate clicked off the TV, disgusted. "Live by the sword, die by the sword," she mumbled. "I'm going for a run."

"You sure?" Kyle asked, looking worried.

"A short run. I'll be fine," Kate said as she went upstairs to get her shoes.

As she headed out the door and down the street, she mumbled out loud over her music, "I hate guns."

Always have always will. Only cowards glorify guns, and only assholes love violence. I ought to know.

Her anger made her run faster.

Twenty minutes later, she was running along Rock Creek where the shade on the trail and the flowing water made it seem a little cooler, but Kate slowed down her pace considerably. It was close to noon and already in the high 80s and humid. As she ran, the trail curved around a huge tree. Startled, she realized she was in the spot where she was when she first heard the explosions.

Not explosions.

Gunshots.

Had so many people with guns really been that close to her? It was a city after all, with houses near, all hidden by the trees and woods of Rock Creek Park. It seemed more people had guns in their homes than she would have ever thought.

Today, the usually active path was very quiet. Not even a bird was singing. She hadn't seen another soul since she transitioned from paved road to dirt trail. She slowed to a stop and looked around, noticing that her hands were shaking, and she suddenly felt very anxious.

Probably PTSD. It might be better to run in the streets today.

Suddenly, she saw a flash of white. Her body flew into the air, moving so fast that her stomach entered her mouth and she gagged. The air went from sweltering to icy cold. She couldn't see anything except white light until she abruptly stopped.

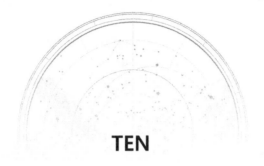

TEN

Two Days After the Shooting

K ate was in a white room. She felt unsteady standing, so she squatted down on the floor. Gulping for air, she tried to tame the major nausea that overcame her. She sat down hard and pulled her legs in, sitting cross-legged and gulping. She tried to control herself, thinking she must look like a fish gulping for air or a cat trying to puke up a hairball.

The room felt very cold after the heat and humidity of outside.

"What the hell?" she gagged out, teeth chattering.

Had she been drugged? Kidnapped? Tossed in a refrigeration truck?

"The world has gone insane. I give up," she said out loud as her gagging subsided. She made herself smaller and wrapped her arms around her body for warmth. Only then did she really look around.

The walls, floor, and ceiling were all white, making it hard to tell how large the room was. She thought she was alone. She was very cold, shivering from head to toe.

"Hello? Where am I? Who are you? Why have you kidnapped me? Are you going to kill me?" she yelled, feeling frantic. "Fine, just do it! What's it going to be? With a virus or a bullet?" Silence. "Come on! What is this? Some brand new 2020 Hell? You're not original! This seems like a cliché science-fiction movie!" She was becoming more and more hysterical—and scared—with each word.

Suddenly, Barack Obama appeared a few feet away.

Kate jumped up, so startled she almost peed. She was squeezing her legs together like a five-year-old and shivering. "What the hell?"

President Obama just stared at her.

"What's going on?" Kate asked, her voice shaking.

"You are Kate," said President Obama in his normal calm halting voice.

He paused.

Kate shrugged. Waited for more. After a few long moments, she said, "You aren't really President Obama."

"No, I am not," he said very slowly.

"What do you want from me?" Kate asked. *Why is my kidnapper pretending to be Obama?*

"You need to do something. It's very important. You need to tell your leaders that what happened was just a warning. More violence will come," he said so slowly. It was like he had to think really hard for each word, or he was a machine.

"What are you talking about? More violence? My leaders?" Kate said, confused.

Suddenly, she was in the dark, moving so fast, terrified. She landed on the trail softly, but she was so startled that she stepped backward, almost falling down the wooded slope into the creek. Catching her balance and looking over her shoulder at the boulders below in the creek, she thought maybe more violence had started.

"What was that? Did that really happen?" Kate whispered out loud. She touched her head, looking for a bump before bolting for home.

And I voted for him, Kate thought, sprinting down the trail.

ELEVEN

Two Days After the Shooting

Kate ran into her house, up the stairs, and threw herself on the bed. Kyle had not said a word, so she assumed he was out walking.

Was she going crazy? Was that a hallucination? Should she call a therapist for an emergency session? No, surely, she just blacked out on the trail and dreamed the rest. It was too hot. She hadn't eaten enough. She was dehydrated. She hadn't been sleeping. Her usual anxiety was amplified.

The mass shooting this week was just another weird thing to happen in 2020. Another weird thing that she, and everyone on the planet, would be expected to normalize and eventually move on from and pretend like never happened. Just like the pandemic. Just like the economic collapse that lost more women their jobs than men and hurt the poor while the rich got richer. Everything was a mess, and there was so much heartbreak and sadness and violence. And women always bore more pain and suffering. Always.

Her mind was jumping around incoherently. She began crying from the emotional overload.

It didn't happen. Anyway, who would lock her in a room with a Cyborg Barack Obama? What kind of cruel joke was that? No, she'd totally made it up like the crazy dreams she had after drinking too much wine.

Curled in a ball, she bawled for thirty minutes straight. She cried for many reasons, but mostly because she feared she was losing her mind.

Eventually, she sat up, her body feeling gross. She realized she had been sweating, freezing, sweating again, and was now cold and covered in tears, slobber, and snot.

She heard the front door open, and she rushed into the bathroom to shower. Kyle didn't need to see her like this.

TWELVE

Two Days After the Shooting

Kate bounded down the stairs, clean and refreshed, and headed to her computer to work. She had decided to forget the whole experience on the trail. She'd made it up. It was a figment of her overactive imagination.

"How was your run?" Kyle asked.

"Totally fine. Hot. Short. Uneventful. There was no inexplicable kidnapping. No terrifying flight into a white room with President Obama," Kate said, laughing nervously.

"Cool?" Kyle said the word like a question, heading to his computer.

Kate stared at her computer, trying to read spreadsheets and contracts. Even though she didn't have to work until Monday, work would be a good distraction. But after a few minutes of blankly staring at the screen, she gave up. She picked up a pen and paper and started writing with the intention of ripping up her thoughts afterward like her old high school journals that she'd destroyed.

Two Days After The Shooting

<u>Things That Happened</u>
<u>Today on My Run</u>

It was hot, so I passed out on the trail.

It was hot, I tripped, and hit my head and passed out.

I just fainted for no reason. It happens.

It was some kind of joke. A pandemic joke.

Maybe I was on camera, but since I was not funny, they did not ask me to sign paperwork. Or maybe I am online right now on some terrible mean comedy show? Me, panting and shaking, in a white room looking terrified, so people can laugh.

Social media can be vicious, Kate thought, but did not write down this idea.

She started to write again, adding to her list.

Drugs can't be involved. I think I would know. I don't even feel drunk.

Why would President Obama warn me that more violence will come?

Wait, tell me to warn leaders more
violence will come?

What leaders????????????????????????

What violence?????????????????????????????????

I lost my mind today. The pandemic stress and the mass shooting got me.

Kate reread the list of things that happened today a few times, shaking her head affirmatively.

"Yep, that's it. I captured it," she said quietly to herself.

Then she slowly ripped the paper into tiny pieces.

She started a search for "woman in park running and freaking out."

After many different searches, Kate felt confident she wasn't being punk'd.

At least not yet.

She decided to not think about it again, ever. She had experience with shelving bad memories. In particular, memories that involved guns.

THIRTEEN

Three Days After the Shooting

On Friday morning, the Office of Personnel Management announced that the government would remain closed for another week, excluding essential employees only.

People struggled as they tried to get back to their normal lives after the shooting. Doctors were interviewed on the news, and they just cried or babbled incoherently. It was the same for nurses and emergency front-line personnel. They cried from the stress of processing so much death while mourning their own loved ones. Most police were dead. Millions of Americans were dead.

While eating breakfast and staring at the TV, Kate watched a young TSA agent being interviewed.

"We were fortunate overall that since the pandemic had significantly reduced flights, only a few dozen planes went down. Some captains had a gun in the cockpit; there was also a co-pilot, and generally only one shot themselves. Unfortunately, a few flights had two armed pilots or an armed sky marshal, which caused significant problems to make the plane go down. We lost a lot of passengers and some people on the ground. It could have been way worse. We are investigating each incident to determine exact numbers, identify the dead, and notify their next of kin." Just then, the anchor cut him off to announce breaking news.

Kate almost choked on her cereal, dreading what happened now.

The anchor announced, "The President will be making a statement about the mass shooting soon. This is the first we have heard from him since it happened."

"Wow, like anyone cares what that idiot has to say," Kyle said. He had walked into the room when he heard Kate choking.

"It's so strange that he survived. I assumed he would have a gun. He loves the NRA. Maybe Secret Service doesn't allow it?" Kate said, wiping her face after her coughing fit.

"I doubt he would listen to the Secret Service. He doesn't listen to anyone. He is from New York, and New Yorkers don't own guns," Kyle said like he was an expert.

"Why not?" Kate asked.

"I read that New Yorkers, like all Americans, bought more guns because of the pandemic and protests, but in New York, it takes like a year to get a permit and costs thousands of dollars for the permit, training, and the gun itself. We know the President is cheap with his own money. Besides, he has taxpayers paying for his safety. I'm not surprised he's alive," Kyle continued.

CNN went live to the White House just as the President started to speak, but it didn't look like the White House.

"Is he in the bunker?" Kyle asked, peering at the TV. "That looks like an imitation Oval Office."

"Would make sense," Kate said. "His security detail is probably not as robust."

"My fellow Americans," the President began, eyes moving back and forth like he was reading from a teleprompter, "on Tuesday, July 14th, millions of Americans died by gunshot. We have not yet determined how or why this tragedy occurred. Right now, we are asking Americans to stay home and safe. Check in on loved ones. Help with processing the deceased. Check and see if friends, family, and neighbors have enough to eat and are safe. Half of my Cabinet, including the Vice-President, passed away on Tuesday. We are asking career agency experts to fill acting roles to ensure the government continues to work and serve the people through this crisis. Over a quarter of the US Congress has died, and one party took a far bigger hit than the other. As we work to fill important government roles in all three branches, have faith that we will continue to serve the American people."

At this point the President stopped reading and looked at the camera and said, "We will find out who is responsible and be it a foreign nation, terrorist organization, antifa, or individuals, they will pay. We will do to them what they have done to us. God bless America." He stood up and walked away.

The camera followed the President's back in silence as he left the odd room.

"Definitely not the Oval Office," Kyle said.

A few seconds later, the CNN anchor jumped in. "Well, that was brief and not very helpful. I think we all want information which simply does not exist yet. We have also learned, and were anticipating the President to say, that all three of his adult sons died on Tuesday. His daughter is in the hospital in critical condition as a result of a gunshot wound. These are such sad and tragic times for everyone. We will take a break and ask our expert panel their thoughts on the President's statement when we return."

"Interesting," Kate said to Kyle as she turned down the volume.

"For all their passionate defense of the second amendment and the NRA and lack of action taken by both parties to prevent gun violence, you would have thought more actually owned guns," Kate mused. "Even many Democrats love guns and the NRA. I would have thought the majority of Congress would have had guns. Well, maybe in their home states? Congress was in session, right? So, they would be in D.C. and not with their guns?"

"Makes sense," Kyle responded.

Kate switched channels. FOX was doing a memorial piece on the Vice President and the President's family. It was sad. Even though she despised them, tears rolled down her cheeks. She flipped to MSNBC, and it was just crying people and dead bodies and people blaming the President for the shooting.

The Speaker of the House and Senate leadership were having a joint press conference later, but Kate had no interest in watching it.

She clicked off the TV and left it off the rest of the day.

FOURTEEN

Five Days After the Shooting

O ver the weekend, there were numerous press conferences with local elected officials trying to bring order back. Many governors and lieutenant governors died, so states were struggling to determine succession.

The D.C. mayor announced a city-wide curfew. She also provided information and hotlines to store and move the remaining bodies and how to find professional mental health and other support. Frontline workers in grocery stores and gas stations were interviewed. Many seemed confused by the question, "How are you holding up?" One poor soul, an African immigrant, just kept saying in perfect English to the reporter, "I don't understand the question."

"I think he means he does not understand the point of the question," Kate said to the TV.

The mayor was on the news every few hours looking exhausted. She had lost many friends and colleagues and repeated the same messages. "Please, everyone just get through the day. Focus on today. Eat healthy food and rest; we are all under enormous stress. We are all hurting. Please do not verbally or physically strike out at family or friends; we need kindness and love and support like never before. And please do not touch people except those that live in your home. Continue to wash your hands and wear a mask when outside your home. We are still in a pandemic, and we need to stop the illness and dying."

Throughout the weekend, Kate went about her business. She stayed inside the house, both because the pandemic raged outside, and the nation and world were still reeling from the mass shooting.

She watched the news and called friends and family, eager to find a way to help. Everyone seemed so stressed. There was so much sadness. People said they needed time to mourn. Some said they would schedule zoom funerals when they knew what was happening to loved one's bodies. Facebook and Twitter were awash with death notices.

"Hi, Mom, how's it going?" Kate asked on FaceTime. Her mom's skin looked older, like she'd aged years in the last 24 hours. Even her hair looked older. She had the same thick brown wavy hair as Kate, only shorter and now streaked with gray. Her big brown eyes, so like Kate's, were filled with worry.

"I hate guns, Kate. I have always hated guns. But this is crazy and it's just too much. I still have the kids with me. Leia is easiest since she is in my class and trusts me; she's old enough to understand somewhat. Jake is a mess and keeps crying for his parents. The baby, Katniss, has no idea what is going on; she seems shell-shocked. Luckily, my neighbor has a two-year-old and is helping me remember what is what. Their two dogs and cat are all here together in my two-bedroom condo. It's crazy and too much." Kate's mom responded with a rush of words.

"I can't express enough how ridiculous those names are and yet how much I love them," Kate said, and heard her mom giggle, happy to cheer her up if only for a second. "You're a hero for helping, Mom. Seriously, teachers do too much in the normal world; you're all angels. I wish I was there and could help." Her mom had always been good with kids.

"It's okay. We had to get our students out of houses with dead bodies. Most of us at Northfield Elementary are alive; almost none of us had guns. I guess all the shooter drills just made us hate guns more. Anyway, I sure do wish these kids' parents did not have guns. Can you believe it? Both parents had guns in a house with a fourth grader, kindergartner and toddler? It was an accident waiting to happen. Just insane. We are waiting to clear relatives. Hopefully, that will be done soon. The school should not have this role, but someone needs to look out for all these orphans. We can't hand them over to just anyone," Kate's mom added.

The baby started to cry. "I have to go, Kate. You and Kyle are okay, right? Safe? No virus?" She asked.

"Yes, Mom, we are good. Go take care of Baby Katniss. I love you," Kate said and hung up.

Kyle was sitting on the couch next to Kate listening to her call.

"Kyle, I wish my mom wasn't in Florida. There's too much COVID and too many guns in Florida. She can't even stay inside until things settle down because she is taking care of those kids. I hope she's remembering to wear a mask in this chaos."

"I am sure she is. She is smart and kind. I bet she even gets that baby to wear a mask," Kyle replied.

Kate leaned on Kyle, resting her head on his shoulder.

"The news says COVID hospitalizations were spiking again nationally. Many people had avoided going to the hospitals the first few days after the shooting to allow the medical staff time to focus on gunshot victims—to their personal detriment—a few days of dropped oxygen levels at home could be deadly. Have you talked to your parents today?" Kate asked.

Kyle just nodded.

Kate wanted to go out and visit and hug people, but mostly she sat around staring at the TV or her computer and cried.

"I generally like the mayor and appreciate her soothing words of support and comfort, but it's the words she's not saying that I find concerning," Kate told Kyle. "Social media is full of news about looting and the crime rate exploding because there were no police. People are scared and desperate. Is it true? Is there violence happening? Where? Why doesn't the mayor address that? It could be social media bullshit or exaggerated stories. We are in D.C. and don't see it, right? Where exactly is the looting? Is it fake news out of Russia? And now that we're clear on what happened, a mass suicide, why aren't the reporters asking the mayor or President or any officials *why* the mass suicide happened? Will it happen again?" She thought of Cyborg Barack Obama's message, his warning that there would be more violence.

"I have no idea, Kate. Everything is just so fucked up," Kyle responded. Kate winced at the swearing. "The news doesn't show looting, not even FOX, but they are showing abandoned guns everywhere. Guns left behind where they committed their last crime. Guns tossed in the streets, I assume by relatives of the dead? To get them out of the house? No one wants them now out of fear they will suffer the same fate as the millions who used them on themselves. I saw one in the gutter across the street from our house. Think it was Yvette's?"

Kate just shrugged. "Are local governments going to just leave guns out on the streets?" Kate asked Kyle.

The thought of seeing guns around every day made her nauseous.

"I don't know, but it's a sign of the times that no one wants to assume ownership," he replied. "People are either terrified of guns now or angry with them."

Kyle turned up the volume as an anchor introduced some expert. "Watch this. I saw this interview earlier. It's interesting."

"We have some additional information about the timeline last Tuesday. We know people shot themselves with their own guns. Most were within the first five minutes. Multiple guns being fired simultaneously mimicked the sound of explosions. Some people had to locate and load their weapon, so additional shots were heard a couple of minutes later. Finally, there were stragglers at the end of the time window. Again, if a gun owner was with their gun, they died quickly in the first round of shots. Others had to go get their guns; some drove home from work or went from home to work. Apparently, if it took more than fifteen minutes to locate or retrieve the gun, they were safe. Unfortunately, due to the pandemic, many people were at home with their guns," the expert paused.

"We have interviewed people who seemed to be on their way to get their gun but were not able within the fifteen-minute window. When asked what they were thinking and feeling, they said they could not remember anything, some sort of fugue state. We hope their memories will come back and provide some answers," he continued.

"Very interesting," Kate said.

"Shush. Listen," Kyle said.

"The mass shooting hit some states harder than others. In the cities, law enforcement, gang members, and drug dealers all died in large numbers. Some regular, law-abiding citizens were affected as well. In more rural areas, gun ownership is more common, regardless of profession. Some towns were completely devastated, and there are many orphans across the country. Since most public health departments and social services have been in funding crisis due to years of neglect, and now with the burden of the pandemic, it has made this new crisis that much harder to address. Fortunately, many good Samaritans are jumping in and helping," the expert continued.

"Like your mom," Kyle said as he got up and left the room.

"Who is this expert?" Kate asked loudly, so Kyle could hear her in the other room. "She seems to know a lot. Must be with Homeland Security? Maybe Health and Human Services? What agencies are in charge?"

Kate continued to project her voice into the kitchen. "I saw the Virginia Governor explaining why we have not had electricity disruptions. Apparently, oil platforms and nuclear facilities have armed security details, and many of those people shot themselves. However, the engineers and technicians can't have weapons at the facilities. If they did own personal guns at home and could not get to them, well, we are fortunate to have enough employees alive maintaining our infrastructure. But maybe a lot of essential employees died at home? Maybe people are working 24/7 to hold us all together. We should definitely find a way to show our appreciation to them like we have for doctors and nurses due to COVID. Damn, I feel so useless while so many are working really hard and others totally struggling," Kate said.

"Here, drink," Kyle said, returning with a glass of wine.

"Thank you," Kate said before taking a sip, feeling very lucky for all her privilege.

Lucky to have a job that she could do from home.

Lucky none of her friends with kids had left them orphaned.

Lucky to be with a man who didn't need to prove his masculinity by owning a gun.

FIFTEEN

Eight Days After the Shooting

A week had passed since Kate had last gone on a run. She tried not to think about the white room or Obama since she ripped the paper into tiny pieces. She tried to bury the experience deep in her mind, but the more she ignored it, the more it crept back in.

Kate was lying in bed. She did not know what day it was, or even what time, though it seemed to be getting dark. Mostly she watched TV or scrolled through social media, addicted to the gruesome news. She had constant background anxiety that she was losing her mind.

"Are you sure you don't want to run today, babe?" Kyle asked, sitting at the foot of the bed. "It's cooling down. I'll go with you. It will make you feel better."

"Do you really think that we can have PTSD, even if we didn't lose anyone important to us?" Kate asked.

He squeezed her calf. "Of course, we have PTSD! These are very stressful times. Between the shooting and pandemic, we're all feeling overwrought. Why?"

"Nothing," she said, closing her eyes. She'd cracked, right? She'd made up a crazy weird experience as a coping mechanism.

"I think I have just the thing for you." He got up and left the room. She pulled out her phone and googled: "Can hallucinations happen to people under stress?"

Yikes. Maybe she needed to speak to a therapist about it.

"Here you go," Kyle handed her a wine goblet filled higher than normal. She could tell by the smell wafting under her nose that it was her favorite Pinot Noir, the one they usually saved for special occasions.

She scooted over to make room for Kyle to sit on the edge of the bed. He had a beer and clinked it against her glass. "You know, starting next week, we go back half-time."

"When did OPM announce that?" she tensed, thinking about her spreadsheets and accounts and the battle to protect Space Force funding from the Wall. She wondered if what happened would make people less or more desirous of the 20-foot, thousand-mile monstrosity?

"Just saw an alert," he said. "But I was thinking, since we're slowly easing back into work, maybe we can find something useful to do with our free time."

"No one wants our blood." Kate sighed.

"I know. And I know being cooped up in this house with constant tragic news is not good for our mental health. I know attending church isn't your thing, but I saw on the neighborhood listserv that they're calling for volunteers; they need help calling members to check in and find out what, if anything, is needed. It's been just over a week and needs are shifting," Kyle said.

Kate thought about the pets that didn't have owners anymore and children who'd lost one or both parents.

"Anyway, it might feel nice to do something productive. For other people. For our community," he said, taking a swig.

Yes. Kate needed to be productive. She needed to do something other than hide in bed drinking good wine and questioning her sanity.

SIXTEEN

Nineteen Days After the Shooting

"**S**trange that it's still July," Kyle said as they lay in bed. "This has been the longest month in the longest year ever," he continued, half awake.

"It's not July anymore," Kate said, almost laughing. Her eyes were still closed. "I'm pretty sure it's August. I think it's the first or maybe second."

"Oh. The days really do run together now. It is Sunday, right?" Kyle sounded a little concerned by his absentmindedness.

Kate opened her eyes and focused on a calendar hanging on the wall. "Yes. Sunday. We don't work today. It's Sunday, August 2nd," she said to sooth his anxiousness.

She rolled over on him and kissed him. They had not had sex since right after the shooting. They both had fallen into a depression, followed by a compulsion to stay busy with volunteer work to try and not think or feel.

She crossed her arms on his chest, looked right into his eyes and kissed him.

"Kyle, I still don't feel like having sex. It's weird. I have never felt like this for so long. I think it's all the sadness and stress."

"I think sex would help us both with the stress. Make us feel better," Kyle said, leaning up for another kiss.

Kate laughed, rolled off him, and stood up.

"I finally feel like going for a run again. My muscles are agitated and need to move," Kate said. She had not felt like running since her hallucination, and she really missed it.

"Maybe getting blood into your legs will help it go elsewhere," Kyle said in a serious voice.

Kate laughed again. "It can't hurt!"

"Don't run long. It's supposed to be near 100 today. Hot already," he added as he flipped over to go back to sleep.

Kate dressed, brushed her teeth, and smeared on sunblock. She was humming to herself, excited for a run. She put on sunglasses, a mask, and grabbed her iPod. She never ran with a phone; it was her time to unplug from the world. However, standing on the porch, seeing what she assumed was Yvette's discarded gun still on the street, she hesitated and considered going back in for her phone.

"Having a phone would not have made any difference," she mumbled to herself. She refused to believe the hallucination would happen again. She had buried that deep, like a nightmare or a brief mental breakdown. She was finally feeling better and safe.

She didn't need her phone.

She started jogging down her street.

Kate planned to stay on the roads but absentmindedly found herself on the trail. There was shade and it was cooler. It was barely eight in the morning and already hot and muggy. She was heading down the trail toward the water. Several runners were also out on the trail, lulling her into a false sense of security.

She approached the spot where she was deposited after being in the white room with Obama, and she stopped abruptly. Another runner almost ran into her from behind.

"Sorry!" Kate exclaimed as the runner diverted past her. The runner kept going, so Kate shouted, "Seriously, that was so rude! Really sorry!"

She turned around laughing, embarrassed about the collision that she almost caused. She started to run again, heading back home, when it happened.

Just like before.

She saw a white flash.

Her body flew into the air.

Again, the speed made her stomach enter her mouth and she almost vomited. The air went from sweltering to icy cold. She couldn't see anything except white light until she abruptly stopped in the cold, white room.

This time she sat down immediately to avoid falling. She wrapped her arms around her knees against the painful cold. She looked around and yelled, "God dammit," through chattering teeth as she ripped off her mask. "What the fuck is happening? Now you are making me swear, and that is making me very angry!" Her voice cracked as she yelled, not used to screaming.

Kate put her head on her knees and started to really shake. This was actually happening, she realized with a big, frustrated sigh. It wasn't a dream. It wasn't a nightmare. It wasn't her imagination or a hallucination.

When she opened her eyes, President Obama was standing 20 feet away.

In his halting and very slow speech he said, "Kate, you have failed. You have not told your leaders that this was a warning, and there will be more violence. Soon."

Kate cleared her voice and said, "I don't understand. Where am I? Who are you? What leaders? What violence? Why me? Why President Obama?"

Her voice became shriller with each question. She was shaking, almost stuttering. She was angry and scared and very, very cold.

President Obama just stared at her.

After a couple of minutes, Kate noticed she stopped shivering. The room wasn't as cold.

She stopped squeezing her knees and leaned back, sitting cross-legged.

She and President Obama seemed locked in a staring contest. Kate was determined to not say a word until she got answers.

After a couple more minutes in awkward silence, she realized it was really getting warmer. She stood up without taking her eyes off his.

Her voice cracked when she spoke, just from nerves now and not cold. "Send me back. If you won't answer my questions, this is pointless, so let me leave," she told Obama.

He didn't say a word, but his form changed.

He turned into Kyle.

Kate's heart almost exploded from fear. She had no idea what was happening, or why, but it terrified her to be staring at Kyle.

"What, what, what," she said incoherently as tears welled up in her eyes.

He suddenly morphed back into Obama.

Then he became the Pope.

Kate was crying and shaking in fear and confusion. She generally supported all religions and considered herself very spiritual but seeing the Pope made her think of child rape; it did not give her any comfort.

His form kept changing from rock stars to the D.C. mayor to her boss and finally an animal.

A large orange tabby cat was now sitting across from her.

Kate almost laughed. She recognized him as Rex, a chubby sweet Cheeto she'd fostered last year. He only stayed with her and Kyle for a few weeks. He was quickly adopted because of his big personality. He always had an intelligent and very satisfied look on his face. He could be a cuddly goofball. Rex was the perfect cat.

This version did not seem scary at all, even though he was six feet tall.

"So now you're Rex?" Kate asked.

"Yes," Rex answered.

A huge talking Rex in this white room made her laugh. "I'm losing my mind, Rex," Kate told the cat.

"I will send you back. You have five days to tell your leaders this violence was just a warning and more is coming. I will know when you speak to them.

Five days." He spoke in a voice that Kate thought was exactly how Rex would have sounded if he spoke.

She cocked her head in disbelief. She was so focused on this bizarre occurrence, a large talking cat giving her a cryptic message, that she couldn't drum up a response.

A sudden sensation overcame her, and she realized she was going to be sent back.

"Wait!" she screamed. "What leaders? I don't know any leaders. I think you picked the wrong person," she said fast and loud in a panic.

The sensation stopped, and she took a deep breath.

"I am serious, Rex. I don't know any leaders. This is D.C.; pick the President or the mayor or someone with power. I don't know anyone. I wish I could help stop the violence. I really do. I hate violence. I mean, I assume you are talking about the mass shooting? Wait, do you know what caused the mass shooting?" Kate paused for an answer.

Rex just stared at her.

After another silent staring contest, Rex said, "Tell the leaders at Space Force. Tell the leaders who travel in space that there will be more violence. You have five days."

With that, Kate hit the trail hard, but this time nailed a firmly planted superhero landing.

SEVENTEEN

Nineteen Days After the Shooting

Kate stood up, relieved she did not risk falling into the creek this time. "Weird," she said out loud. "Oh, shit," she added more intensely and swiftly ran home. When she arrived, she flung the door open and slammed it behind her. She ran up the stairs, stripped off her clothes, and mumbled, "What the hell?"

"What's up?" Kyle asked, entering the bedroom. "Oh! The run worked," he exclaimed with pure joy, misinterpreting her energy. "I love morning sex!" He started taking off his shirt and jumped into bed.

"No way, Kyle. I saw something on the trail. Something totally messed up," Kate said, walking into the bathroom and turning on the shower. She kicked the bathroom door shut so hard that it slammed loudly.

She took a long shower, trying to figure out what to say and do. How much should she reveal to Kyle?

Rex had said: "Tell the astronauts at Space Force that there will be more violence."

This showed how little Rex knew about Space Force or leadership in the government. There were no astronauts at Space Force, at least not yet. The astronauts worked for NASA.

Kate stared at the suds running down the drain and said out loud, "Rex did not say astronauts. Rex said tell the leaders at Space Force. 'Tell the leaders who travel in space that there will be more violence. You have five days.' Remember it correctly, exact."

Kate finished in the bathroom and walked out, slamming the door again as a wave of anger rushed over her. Why had Rex chosen her? She wasn't even senior management at Space Force and hadn't worked there long. She didn't know anyone in authority well enough to convey this kind of message. What if they thought she was crazy?

Kyle was still lying on the bed, his armed crossed beneath his head. "Kate, what did you see?"

"Space Force confuses everyone. Few people know its purpose and the public considers it a joke. There's a sitcom about it!" she snapped.

"I know," Kyle responded. His voice remained calm and his demeanor patient, even though he looked very confused by the direction of the conversation.

"I would have preferred to stay at NASA. NASA has a storied history. NASA has accomplished so many firsts. NASA changed the world for the better. NASA brought the world together in powerful ways, through hope and celebration of science and innovation and courage. NASA brought together sworn enemies. Russia hosts American manned launches," Kate vented, pacing around the bedroom.

"I know, babe. What happened on your run? Was it on the street or trails? Are you okay?" Kyle tried to redirect her.

Kate continued pacing. "NASA brought together corporate innovation and investment with government expertise to create the perfect symbiotic relationship. NASA brings the best of the best from the military branches to work for a civilian agency that benefits all mankind. Space Force is a branch of the military for war in space. Its violent intentions are ridiculous! And hopefully unnecessary." Kate's voice trailed off.

"Okay, Kate. What happened out there? I'm worried. Did you see something violent? A gun? Did you see people without masks? Were you harassed? Harassed by people without masks?" Kyle's voice grew louder as he speculated.

Kate stomped downstairs, and Kyle jumped up and followed.

In the kitchen, she opened and closed the refrigerator a few times, absently looking at the shelves.

"Hungry?" Kyle asked, trying hard to be patient.

Kate grabbed one of Kyle's beers and popped it open. Kyle's eyes opened wide. Kate rarely drank beer and never in the morning. Never.

She walked into the living room and sat down, taking a few big swigs. Some of the beer went up her nose and came shooting out. She just wiped it away with the back of her hand.

"Tell me what happened, Kate. Please," Kyle said, sitting down next to her.

Kate had still not decided what to say or what not to say. She had a terrible time lying. Lies got stuck in her throat and made her feel sick. Best to be as truthful as possible. The beer was helping.

"I saw someone, or something, on the trail very near to where I was when the shooting started. I think they were insane, or PTSD'ed, or on drugs, or a combination. I don't know," Kate said.

Kyle nodded his head to encourage her to continue but did not interrupt.

Kate sighed and then burped. Horrified, she covered her mouth.

Kyle shook his head impatiently. "Go on, Kate."

Kate hesitated. She wanted Kyle to believe her. If what the mirage of Barack/Rex said was true, she didn't have time to waste proving that she wasn't crazy. "He said, well, he warned me, there will be more violence. He told me to tell the authorities at Space Force that there will be more violence. I know it's crazy. I know he was crazy, but with so many crazy things happening it just seemed, I don't know, concerning," Kate said. "I think I should tell someone."

Kate winced, remembering how she told someone about Theo and his duffle bag of weapons. She looked straight at Kyle, watching him to see humor or incredulousness in his face, but there was none.

"Of course. Who should you tell? Police are useless now with so few of them. And it wasn't really a crime, per se. Maybe tell the mayor's office? Report it as harassment? Was he wearing a mask? Or, who knows, maybe he knows something about the shooting? God knows no one seems to know what the hell happened on July 14. So, maybe the FBI? Those two we saw on the local news? I guess they were the only agents in

America that did not own guns. They didn't seem too bad." Kyle was trying to be helpful. "We can track them down. I mean, even if this guy you talked to is just a crack-raddled nutbag, they should look into it," Kyle said.

Kate took the last big swig of the beer. "No. We have to think bigger. Think different. Who do I still know at NASA?"

EIGHTEEN

Nineteen Days After the Shooting

While Kyle was talking, it suddenly dawned on Kate that Space Force was a branch of the military. *Live by the gun, die by the gun.* Whatever Rex was doing, responding with the guys who got off on war and violence would not be helpful. She preferred to not involve them, but Rex specifically said Space Force.

Space Force does not even go into space yet.

"I am sure your people at Space Force know people at NASA. You know people at NASA. Do you want to go that route? I get what was said, but maybe local officials or FBI is better. I think they can deal with druggie, mentally ill harassers better than NASA. I bet they can tell if he is a threat or not. I doubt Space Force has that kind of expertise, even if they are military," Kyle responded.

Kate sighed. "I prefer not to talk to Space Force. I don't want to engage Space Force. If I speak to anyone at NASA, they'll think I'm reaching out on official Space Force business. I need to talk to someone off the record. Like a scientist or someone involved with launches." Her mind was moving a mile a minute. "I'm pretty sure it's best to stay away from policy staff or analysts for now. And definitely not political hacks." She took the empty beer bottle to the kitchen. "All I have to do is warn them. What they do with the information is on them. I will have done what was asked. Hopefully, that'll be enough." Kate opened the refrigerator and reached for another beer.

Kyle raised his eyebrows when Kate walked back into the living room with a second beer. "Are you still that upset?" he asked. "I know the dude freaked you out, but seriously, with the coronavirus and mass shooting, people are cracking up. Don't let one scary guy on the trail turn you into a beer drinker," he joked.

Kate giggled, feeling a bit tipsy. "If I am still upset after this one, I promise to switch to wine."

"Good. Not sure I could handle anymore big changes this year. Throw me over the edge," Kyle continued.

"Sinclair!" Kate shouted, startling Kyle.

"What about him?" Kyle asked.

They had only seen Sinclair once since they took Yvette to the hospital. He had stopped to thank them for their help and said he was working with the family to plan a funeral. He said he felt bad that he had been traveling for work when the shooting happened. Kate and Kyle try to reassure him there was nothing he could have done. No one knew why the shooting happened on that particular day.

"Sinclair works for NASA," said Kate.

"How do you know that?" Kyle asked.

Kate's cheeks flushed. "We discussed it once. We had both finished a run. Just neighbor chitchat. It was when we first moved in here. I think he said he worked on launches at NASA. I said I had also worked for NASA, managing contracts for a brief time, before being moved to Space Force. He didn't seem particularly impressed. You know, like anyone important who works directly on missions acts when speaking to a contract manager. You get what I mean," Kate said excitedly, hopeful that Sinclair was the key to getting Rex's message in the right hands. She put down the beer. "I'm going over there. Hope he's home."

"Seriously? You're just going to knock on his door? Early in the morning, smelling like beer? Tell him some crazy person told you there might be more violence? I doubt he's even home. Remember, his wife died there on the floor. Why would he stay there?" Kyle was incredulous. "If something had happened to you, I couldn't stay here."

Kate's face grew hot. "Where would he go? No one's moving now. We saw him, what, two weeks ago? Okay, maybe he's staying with friends or family? But we are still in a pandemic..." Kate's voice petered off. "Anyway, I won't know if I don't go over there."

As Kate jogged across the street, she saw Sinclair's car was parked in front of his house. She knocked loudly on his door. *People need time to get a mask*, she thought, impatiently pacing as she waited. A minute or so later, he opened the door.

"Hi, Sinclair. How are you doing? I should have come over sooner to see if you needed anything. Again, I'm so sorry about Yvette." Kate talked quickly, like she always did when she was nervous.

I hope he does not realize that I've been drinking.

"Hi, Kate. No problem. Everything is so screwed up, no one knows what to do when someone dies anymore," Sinclair said as he walked out of his house, closing the door behind him. He took a few steps away and leaned on his porch railing.

Kate stepped back down the stairs, making sure they were at least six feet apart.

"Thanks again for your and Kyle's help. Not sure I was thinking clearly. I had no idea what to do," he said.

"Jeez, I wish we could have done more." Kate's eyes welled up, realizing how much pain Sinclair must be in. He'd lost his wife, his best friend, just a few weeks ago in such a shocking way. Tears started flowing. "I am sorry. Not sure why I am crying."

"That's okay. How about you and Kyle? Lose anyone in the shooting?" Sinclair asked.

"No, we were really lucky. We lost a few colleagues but no one we directly loved. It's strange given how many guns there are in America." Kate hoped Sinclair did not think she was judging Yvette.

"I had forgotten Yvette even had that gun. She'd had it since we met. Kept it while we dated and after we married. She said she wasn't going to be a victim. She grew up in a rough neighborhood with a lot of crime. I thought it was badass of her when we were younger. I had never had a gun but thought she was cool. You know, willing to defend and protect herself.

She had it in a lock box that moved from house to house with us. I forgot it was even there," he explained.

"I'm so sorry," Kate said.

"When we first moved from Florida to California, I remember asking her how she would get to it quickly. How would she unlock the box and protect herself?" Sinclair smiled sadly. "She had some long, convoluted explanation that made no sense. Like most gun owners, a whole lot of feelings and very little logic about her gun. As the years went by, I just forgot she had it," he said again.

Kate stayed quiet and let him talk. Tears rolled down her cheeks and under her mask. *Guns only cause violence.* As she thought that, Rex's face entered her mind, and her heart began to race.

"Obviously, now I wish we had gotten rid of it," Sinclair said.

"I am so sorry, Sinclair." Kate couldn't think of what else to say. She could not interrupt his story to say she was upset because she had been harassed in the park. That not only sounded insane but totally insensitive.

"We're going to do a Zoom memorial service next month. I planned to have it when we knew more about why it happened. But as time goes by, I wonder when, if ever, we'll know. No one has claimed responsibility. They can't seem to figure out why it happened or what purpose it served," Sinclair said. "I've called lots of people: Yvette's boss, her friends, funeral home, insurance companies, credit card companies, her gym." He paused, stroking his chin, seeming to think if he needed to call anyone else. "I would say, I'm sorry to tell you that Yvette is dead. There would always be a long awkward pause, followed by the question, by gun or virus? People want to know, you know. And I have to explain the gun," Sinclair said

Kate tried to take deep breaths and stop the tears. How was her being here helping this man? How could she casually ask him if he still worked at NASA? She wanted to hug him. She wanted to show him human compassion. "It must be really hard. I want to hug you so much," she said through sobs. "I did not know Yvette well, but she seemed like a nice, cool person. I can't imagine your pain. Or I can, and it really hurts."

She wanted to say, *I wish I could take away your pain,* but she knew that was a stupid, unhelpful sentiment. Knowing she could do absolutely nothing to help alleviate Sinclair's pain was too much. So, she defaulted to cliches. "I am so sorry for your loss, Sinclair. Let me know if you need anything. Anything at all." She stumbled down the last porch steps and jogged across the street, embarrassed and upset.

NINETEEN

Twenty-Two Days After the Shooting

K ate researched every angle regarding the latest thinking about the cause of the mass shooting. She mostly found crazy religious theories and ridiculous conspiracies given life when repeated by the President. CNN didn't help by airing them. Just that morning, the President had tweeted or retweeted nonsense 65 times.

Mass suicide shootings Actually ANTIFA working with BLACK LIVES MATTER to MURDER Innocent Americans

Has Anyone checked on where @davidhog and other paid actors who Claim to be Victims of school Shootings were that day?

Where was Wicked Hillary? #LOCKHERUP

Kate fell down the rabbit hole of ignorant comments. How could so many Americans—or were they Russian bots—believe this bullshit? The President and his supporters seemed very confident of someone's responsibility, while offering no proof or explanation of how they accomplished this worldwide bloodbath.

However, since so many of the President's supporters had died in the shooting, their crazy claims, while frustrating, were also really sad. Often, while a conspiracy believer was explaining the blame was with Black Lives Matter, Marjorie Stoneman Douglas survivors, or liberals, they would break down crying and say how they had lost parents, kids, partners, and friends in the shooting. It was heartbreaking to watch. And horrifying when they would get back to blaming others while accepting zero responsibility for their loved ones who had the guns and shot themselves.

Time was running out. She spent two days on useless research and now had just three days left to deliver the message. She looked into leadership at NASA, and reluctantly, Space Force, to see if she could find someone to discuss her encounter. She read resumes, bios, press clips, interviews, and official releases, but no one jumped out as the right person. She laughed when she realized she was looking for a person that was brilliant, well-educated, respected in their field, *and* believed in UFOs, life on other planets, and was confident enough in their beliefs to include all that in their bio.

It was Wednesday morning, and Kate was now trying to put it all out of her mind and do her day job work. She stared at her spreadsheets for an hour and accomplished nothing.

She wasn't exactly sure at what moment the five days would expire. She saw, or imagined, Rex on Sunday. Did she have exactly five days, meaning Friday morning? Or five full days, with the clock running out on Friday night? If she did not do as he said, would the violence begin immediately? Would it be more shootings? Kate thought about the guns tossed everywhere and the one in the gutter across the street. Not even the conspiracy believers seemed to want to touch them or pick them up. Maybe on Friday, you wouldn't need to be a gun owner, just near a gun.

What if she picked it up? Or Kyle? Or Sinclair? Neighbors up and down the street had little kids who rode their bikes on the mostly traffic-free street. What if one of them was near it when the moment struck? The terrifying thought made Kate snap out of her scattered depression.

Sinclair had to help. She had to try one more time to talk to him.

Kate knocked loudly on his door and paced back and forth on Sinclair's small front porch. A couple of minutes later, she heard the door being unlocked.

He walked out with a NASA face mask on. Kate took that as a good sign.

"Hi Kate. How are you today?" Sinclair asked.

"Hi Sinclair. I'm good. As well as can be expected." Kate shrugged. "Sorry I rushed off on Sunday. I don't handle death or heartbreak well."

"No worries. None of us do. It doesn't seem to be one of those things we get better at handling with practice. Quite the opposite. Anyway, it should not be this common," Sinclair responded. "So, what's up?"

"Do you have a few minutes? I had a bizarre experience recently and I want to bounce it off someone who I think would understand," Kate explained.

Sinclair squinted his eyes and peered at her house.

"I did tell Kyle, well some of it anyway. But he doesn't work in the space industry, so he doesn't have much … imagination?"

"Okay, sure. What happened?" Sinclair asked, leaning on his porch railing. He seemed more relaxed, like he was happy to talk shop. "I do have a Zoom at eleven," he added, checking his watch.

"First, what exactly do you do at NASA? I think you told me, so I apologize for forgetting. Are you a biophysicist? Did I remember that right?" she asked.

"Yes. I do research for NASA. Yvette worked with the launch program; for a while, we moved frequently for NASA, including to California, Texas, Florida. Here in D.C., she still did some hands-on work in Virginia on launches. I just do research," he explained.

"Research on what?" Kate asked.

"Mostly on things that our astronauts or equipment bring back to Earth," he responded.

Does he mean rocks and debris? Is he being purposefully vague? Does he think too much detail will bore me? Or are the specifics of his work confidential? Kate wondered.

"I've always been intrigued by space and the space program. I'm not smart enough to be any kind of physicist or astronaut, but I loved working for NASA, contributing in my own small way. I was really upset when

I got moved to contracts at Space Force. I wanted to help with research and exploration, not weaponizing space," Kate explained, hoping he would open up more about his work if he understood her better.

"Yes, I hear that from a lot of the employees that were transferred to Space Force, people at all levels. Maybe the next administration will set things right. If we're lucky enough to get a different administration," he added.

His phone called his attention, and he pulled it out of his pocket and looked at it for a few seconds. "Would you hang on a minute, Kate?" he asked. "I'll be right back."

He went into his house and Kate paced some more. She realized they had been standing rather close. Closer than six feet. Good thing they were wearing masks. Her mask read "gratitude" in rainbow colors. She liked her masks to be positive in these dark days.

She thought about what Sinclair had said. She knew more about him than she let on. She had googled him. She knew he was well-educated, probably brilliant with all those degrees, but he was never in the press. His research seemed to fly under the radar, perhaps intentionally.

Of course, the government kept a very short leash on employees at every level and every agency in regard to the press. That was especially true if they studied things that came from space, which she supposed could include Rex.

Sinclair walked out of the house carrying a cup of coffee. "Sorry about that," he said. "So, what was your bizarre experience exactly?"

Kate felt a rush of panic. She figured she might have less than 42 hours if Rex was serious about his threat. She took a deep breath and started slowly. "I was running on a trail in the park and someone grabbed me and said, *'You have five days to tell your leaders this violence was just a warning and more is coming. I will know when you speak to them.'*" Kate stared at Sinclair, watching his reaction.

He just stood there passively, looking at her, but not saying anything.

The uncomfortable silence made Kate fill in more details.

"He specifically said tell the leaders at Space Force. 'Tell the leaders who travel in space that there will be more violence.' He said I had five days, but that was three days ago. I have about 42 hours left if I'm calculating his warning right." Kate's voice trailed off.

As she said it, it all sounded extremely ridiculous, and she was embarrassed.

"Okay," Sinclair said, realizing that was the bizarre incident. He sighed, pulled his mask aside, and took a long sip of his coffee. "Listen, Kate, everyone is under enormous stress. There has been so much death, shocking horrific death, and chronic stress. It has gone on for too long: six months of Hell on Earth from the pandemic before the shooting. Millions are dead. We're all cracking a little under the pressure. This guy in the park may have been having his own breakdown. He may have delusions that he caused the mass shooting or been dealing with survivors' guilt," he said, looking at her kindly. "And you are very nice to indulge him."

Shoot. This was not the response Kate wanted.

"Also, the problem is, even if your crazy messenger is right, I work for NASA, not Space Force. You're the one who works for Space Force. Can't you tell him that you spoke to your boss, I mean *'the leader,'* and that you did fulfill his request?" Sinclair asked, smiling.

Kate sighed.

"And maybe stop running in the park for a while. This person could be delusional and dangerous. But if you do encounter him again, for whatever reason, can't you just tell him you took his message to your leadership at Space Force and to NASA?"

Kate noticed a twitch in his jaw, his mouth pressed firmly together. He was struggling not to laugh. He was indulging her, kind of playing along.

He stayed quiet, sipping his coffee, waiting for Kate to say something.

She decided she liked his angle, even if he was kind of joking. It was actually really helpful. She didn't have to convince him—or anyone—the story was real. And she could still fulfill Rex's request. Sure, it was a loophole, but it was a clever loophole. Kate smiled at Sinclair. "That might work," she said, nodding her head.

But what if her boss thought *she* was mentally unhinged and filed a report? Also, what about Rex's comment about "leaders who go into space?" No one in her department was actually doing that. She had to push on.

"The problem, Sinclair, and why I need your help is that Space Force isn't sending anyone into space yet—so far, only NASA has. A few billionaires are working to be the first private citizens soon. If I, a nobody program analyst, contact anyone in leadership, especially astronauts or any leaders in their division, no one would respond. Best case scenario, I might get a response from an administrative support staffer."

And probably flag me to my boss and end my job, Kate thought, but did not say. Even though she hated it, it was still a job with good benefits.

"That might not be enough to 'prevent more violence.' But if you sent an email to a friend in leadership in the space fight program, or better yet *called*, and just said the truth. You have a stressed-out neighbor that was told by a stranger that she was to 'tell the leaders at Space Force, the leaders that travel in space, that there will be more violence,' and you do it before 10 a.m. on Friday, we will have fulfilled the request. Maybe head off some bad event," Kate said with genuine enthusiasm. *How can he say no to that?*

Sinclair just shook his head for a minute, thinking.

"You were with NASA before, right? You were moved to Space Force recently? Don't you still have contacts at NASA who you could reach out to?" Sinclair asked.

"No, everyone in my budget division moved over to Space Force. I was not at NASA long enough to meet anyone in the flight division, much less leadership. So, it would be best if someone with your credentials made a call. Maybe to a friend? Someone who would just listen. Maybe think you were joking?" Kate said encouragingly, afraid he was going to decide to shut this down.

"But what if they think I've lost my mind? I lost my wife in the mass shooting; they might report me for being unstable. Colleagues might worry about me being concerned about some crazy person in the park. They could think if I believe the crazy person, I, too, am crazy and need help. They could put me on administrative leave. You're asking a lot for some message a quack in the park gave you. I'm not sure I should be messing around with this right now," Sinclair said seriously.

Kate completely agreed with all of Sinclair's concerns. These were her concerns as well.

However, she also felt more and more sure Sinclair was the only path forward. "No way that would ever happen, Sinclair. We're in a pandemic. You're just humoring your crazy neighbor by repeating her crazy story. I will be the one that ends up on administrative leave. No one will think you are crazy. You're just being helpful. A really good neighbor. Especially if you talk to someone you trust. Before Friday at 10 a.m., it could make a difference."

Kate needed him to help. She didn't have time to pursue another option. Hell, she did not have another option.

Sinclair glanced at his phone. "Shoot, I am late for my conference call. Time flies when one is talking crazy conspiracies." He laughed, turning and walking into his house. "See you later, Kate. Good luck with all this."

Kate walked across the street to her house, wondering if that was mission accomplished, or if she had just made her neighbor think she was nuts and he was kindly indulging her.

She rushed to her computer. She felt better than when she walked over to Sinclair's. Even if Sinclair did nothing, Kate felt good for taking the risk and speaking to him. She was taking action, rather than just sitting around worrying.

Who knows? Maybe Sinclair is secretly leadership at NASA.

"Regardless of what Sinclair does, my boss is *my* leader and works for Space Force. Let's hope that is enough," Kate mumbled as she typed.

Hi Carol,

Again, I am so sorry for your enormous loss. I can't imagine the heartbreak you are experiencing.

Everything is fine with my accounts. Of course, I am having delays in submissions from some of my accounts, but nothing extreme. It is expected during these difficult times.

I know you have repeatedly said working is helping you in your mourning, or I would not bring this up, but I did have a strange experience recently in my personal life. Since the "request" was regarding Space Force, I thought I would mention it to you.

I was harassed verbally while running in Rock Creek Park. I don't know how this person knew I work for Space Force, but he demanded that I "tell the leaders at Space Force that there will be more violence."

Under normal circumstances, I would assume this was a joke or a mentally ill person with delusions of grandeur. However, since we are living in highly dangerous and stressful times, I wanted to let you and Space Force know this had occurred. Hopefully, it has not happened to any other Space Force employees.

I do not expect you to take any action. I just wanted you to know.

See you at our next virtual staff meeting and please email, text, message, or call if you need anything regarding this or anything else.

Sincerely,
Kate

She read and reread the email and then hit send. She hoped that was enough to satisfy Rex.

She was running out of time.

TWENTY

Twenty-Three Days After the Shooting

K ate slept soundly that night, convinced she'd done all she could considering that she didn't personally know any "leaders who go into space." She hoped that Rex or Fake Obama or whatever it was would realize she was not the person to handle this message.

She mostly hoped there would not be any further violence. Maybe Obama/Rex had approached other Space Force employees, and the powers that be were holding a top-secret meeting to compare messages and notes and strategize a response.

That—or Kate had lost her mind and now her professional reputation, too.

She recalled a therapist telling her that people who questioned their sanity were usually sane. Those who were fully confident that they were being rational and sane were the ones to wonder about.

With the pressure alleviated, she worked her job through the day, taking small breaks and cleaning the house like she presumed most people working from home did. Her house had never been so tidy. In the evening, she put on a mask and jogged to a local organic market and waited in line to enter, respecting all social distancing protocols.

She had not heard from her supervisor, Carol; there was no confirmation whether she had read the email or not, and she found that a little concerning. If nothing else, Kate would have liked Carol to acknowledge it, even if to joke about Kate's crazy imagination. Not that Carol knew her well enough to make a joke like that.

As she waited her turn to go into the store, she started to worry. She had filled Kyle in, minus details like the terrifying abduction, white room, and big cat. She told him she talked to Sinclair—who acted like it was a joke—and emailed Carol, who was being nonresponsive. Kate had sort of solved the problem; she did what she was asked to do. She informed leadership at Space Force and NASA.

Carol is pretty low on the power totem pole. Was it enough to reach out to her?

Kyle's reaction to her emailing Carol had been supportive. "That's great that you told your boss, but whatever you do, stay off the trails. Do not run in the park. Avoid the nutbag completely. In a few weeks, when everything has calmed down, we can run on the trails again."

She was not going near that trail again.

In less than 24 hours, the five-day window would close.

TWENTY-ONE

Twenty-Four Days After the Shooting

After a night of tossing and turning, Kate gave up on sleep and got up early, counting the minutes until it was socially acceptable to pay Sinclair a visit.

Just before 9 a.m., Kate trotted over to Sinclair's house and knocked loudly.

No answer.

Kate scanned their tree-lined street, spying his car in its usual spot under a shady Oak.

She knocked again, bouncing from foot to foot with nervous energy. Kate knocked and waited for five minutes before going home.

"Did you see Sinclair?" Kyle asked when she walked into the kitchen.

She jumped. "God, you scared me."

"No coffee for you, young lady," Kyle said, laughing.

"He didn't answer the door," Kate told Kyle as she poured a cup of coffee, ignoring Kyle's remark. "I didn't sleep well last night."

"I know. I heard you go downstairs and watch TV. Watching the COVID death clock and endless speculation on the shooting will make your insomnia worse. You have to relax. This kind of stress can have long-term effects. I say we do nothing but watch comedies all weekend. No news. No work. No trails with weirdos. Just funny movies," Kyle said.

It sounded good to Kate, assuming they survived this day. She looked at her watch; it was almost 10 a.m. "Did I do enough?" Kate whispered to herself.

In her mind, Kate was thrust back to middle school, hiding in a car, hoping she had done enough to stop the violence.

The memory made her shiver, and she shook her head hard to move it away.

Out the window, the street seemed calm, pandemic empty. No people rushing to the bus stop or walking into town. No kids skipping to school.

Kyle walked up, looked outside, and then looked back at Kate. He looked worried.

"What do you think? Great idea, right? I'll get some wine, some good stuff. Well, cheap good stuff. We can make a pizza and mentally check out of all this bullshit stress," Kyle added.

"It sounds wonderful," Kate said, smiling at Kyle to reassure him.

"Are schools open now? I mean, if the pandemic was not happening. School starts in August, right?" Kate asked to distract her stressed mind. She glanced at the clock, 9:55 a.m. Her heart raced.

"I think it's later in the month," Kyle responded. "I have to start work. Need to do a few hours. Then wine run and movie time." He kissed her cheek.

Why is he so relaxed? Kate's annoyance with him swelled; he wasn't taking this seriously. Her stress was making her agitated.

But then she remembered: she had not told Kyle about the five-day allotment.

Kate continued to stare out the front window, watching for something to happen. Waiting for the violence to begin. She was also watching for signs of Sinclair.

She could see the gun laying in the gutter.

Should she have picked it up? Put it in the garbage?

Kate stood at the window for an hour.

No Sinclair.

No violence.

When she could hear Kyle talking on a Zoom meeting in the kitchen, she turned on the news. She kept the volume down so he wouldn't hear or be disturbed. She was scared they'd report another violent event, but everything just seemed like normal pandemic and post mass shooting bad.

Within a week of the mass shooting, CNN had started a body count clock that ran alongside the COVID death clock but pulled it off after multiple complaints that it was too insensitive and gruesome.

A reporter was interviewing migrants at the U.S./Mexico border.

"As previously reported, there was chaos at the border. Since many border agents died in the mass shooting, the migrants being processed did not know what to do. Thousands of people crossed illegally. It was a chaotic, disorganized mess for a few weeks, but now things have settled down. I asked Jose Rodriguez, a migrant at the border, what his plans were since locating his wife and children. This was his response:"

"We are going home. We came to America for jobs and opportunity and to escape our corrupt government. But mostly, we came to avoid the constant gun violence. The relentless drug and political wars that made our families and children targets for stray bullets. Some were threatened to take a side or be killed. Without police or order, women and children were raped and victimized. But they are all dead. They killed themselves with the weapons they threatened and terrorized us with. I am taking my family home to start a new life in our country. Our new country."

Wow, that is so awesome! She needed a little good news. *Thanks, Mr. Rodriguez,* Kate thought as she clicked the TV off.

She went back to her computer and tried to do work.

"This is insane," she declared ten minutes later. "There is no way I can work." Kate got up to pace, then stared out the window again. Her computer dinged with an incoming message. She ran to wake up the screen, never so happy to see an email from her boss, Carol.

Subject line: Re: Reporting a strange incident

Yes! She responded to my email!
With shaking hands, Kate opened it.

Hi Kate,

Sorry, that happened to you! What an odd thing, right?

We are living in stressful times. That man probably deserves our compassion and sympathy. We have no idea what he may have lost.

Please do me a favor and stay out of the park for a while. And let me know if anything else strange happens regarding Space Force.

See you at the staff meeting next week.

Thanks!
Carol

At first, Kate sat down relieved. She was happy that Carol seemed to take it rather lightly and wasn't concerned about Kate's mental health. It could get awkward if her boss was worried about her.

Then she felt even more relief. So far, no more violence. Kate had done what she was asked. Even if it was kind of a trick, finding and exploiting a loophole, she had informed "leaders" at Space Force and NASA. She suddenly felt exhausted. All the adrenaline in her blood the past few days and lack of sleep caught up to her.

"Mission accomplished," Kate said out loud.

TWENTY-TWO

Twenty-Seven Days After the Shooting

For the rest of the weekend, Kate tried to relax. As Kyle planned, they watched funny movies. She drank too much wine. They blared music and danced in the living room. She ate healthy food. She did *not* watch the news. She did *not* go near the park. She did *not* discuss the bizarre incident again with Kyle. She didn't even check email or look out the window for Sinclair or evidence of violence.

Well, not too many times.

On Monday morning, Kate woke up early and slipped out of her nightgown before curling her body into Kyle's. As Kyle shifted in his sleep, some male instinct must have kicked in, telling him she was nude. Without opening his eyes, he pulled her up on his naked chest, his lips finding hers. They kissed fiercely for several minutes. As their bodies joined together like they had so many times before, Kate couldn't help but think it felt different this time.

Kyle made love like he had been denied sex for weeks, loving every second.

Kate made love like a person that had survived a war unscathed, feeling lucky to her core.

"Well, good morning to you too," Kyle said when it was over, and they lay exhausted and sweaty in the tangled sheets.

Later, as Kate was getting out of the shower, she heard Kyle talking and assumed he was on an early work call.

Dressed and ready to give her work her full attention for the first time in days, she bounced down the steps. Nothing like being alive and COVID-free and great Monday morning sex to signal a good week to come. Kate was relieved to have her natural optimism back.

She jumped when she entered the kitchen. Sinclair was leaning against their stove, drinking a cup of coffee, his mask dangling from one ear.

No one had entered their house for even a minute since the pandemic started.

"Hey Kate. Sorry to startle you," Sinclair said casually.

"What's up?" Kate asked sharply, with her eyes moving between Kyle and Sinclair. "Sorry, I'm not used to other people being in the house."

"I just wanted to say I am relieved we had an uneventful weekend. Seems your crazy harasser conspiracy friend was wrong," Sinclair said.

"Well, let's just hope he's moved on from the area, poor guy," Kyle added.

The tension hanging in the air told Kate that the two had been talking about something else before she entered the room.

Sinclair put down his coffee cup and headed to the front door.

"Sinclair, I did send an email to Space Force management. As a silly precaution like we discussed. Did you communicate with anyone at NASA?" Kate asked, following him.

"I sure did. I talked to a friend about it," Sinclair responded. "As I suspected, he didn't seem impressed or particularly interested. We're all dealing with our own crazy shit, I guess." He shrugged. "See you around. Thanks for the coffee, Kyle."

Sinclair shut the door behind him.

"Weird. That was very weird, right?" Kate asked Kyle as she watched Sinclair cross the street.

"All's well that ends well," Kyle replied, also looking out the window. "And don't worry, babe. He can't have COVID. He said he has not left the house for weeks, pretty much since we took Yvette to the hospital. I asked him if it was awful being in the house without Yvette. He said it was terrible, but they both traveled a lot before the pandemic for work, so he was kind of used to being there without her. Except for groceries and life stuff, he has been home," Kyle said, jumping around from topics.

"But that's not true. He wasn't home on Friday. He didn't answer the door in the morning, and I did not see him return," Kate said, heading to the kitchen for coffee.

"I mentioned that. He asked what you did on Friday morning. Asked if you had gone anywhere. I said you had gone over to his place, but there was no answer when you knocked. He said he must have been in the shower," Kyle added.

Kyle followed Kate into the kitchen and poured himself more coffee.

"Kind of strange, how curious he was about Friday," Kyle said. "Was Friday special? Did I miss something?"

"Nope. Seemed like a regular day in pandemic post mass shooting hell," Kate responded without looking at him.

It is not a lie.

TWENTY-THREE

Thirty-Five Days After the Shooting

A week had passed and everything remained calm. Kate avoided the park. She worked every day. She tried to not watch the news. She felt more confident that the loophole had worked. There had been no large-scale acts of violence.

In fact, there was relative peace in the world.

Everyone, including the seriously reduced remaining standing armies, was still terrified of guns and weapons. Most violent criminals were dead. An eerie detente permeated the world. The occasional mugging or purse snatching actually made the news. CNN was reporting on domestic violence incidents, which still occurred, but without guns. They reported on them because there was so little other violent crime to cover. The world seemed to hold its breath, adjusting to the new norm of less violence.

"Hey, did you see this?" Kate asked and then read to Kyle from the newspaper. "At the southern border, immigrants are reportedly still crossing peacefully into America, but at a way reduced rate compared to before July 14. With the violent gangs many had been fleeing now dead, the urgency to leave and migrate north, has lessened. 'My preference was always to stay in my home country, but not if I couldn't keep my family safe. The situation has changed dramatically. We are going home,' a woman who asked to not be identified said through an interpreter. I will never get tired of these stories. Looks like things are really improving in Mexico and Central America."

"Well, idiot-in-chief is still calling for his wall in a tweet this morning," Kyle said, reading from his phone. "Congress must Approve the Best WALL now before more People come into our Great COUNTRY stealing Our Jobs."

"It's like he doesn't understand what happened, the enormous impact the mass shooting had on the world. Everything has changed. That tweet is ridiculous," Kate replied. "Of course, he may have just totally lost it. Do narcissists mourn? He never seems to have any feelings or empathy about the plight of the migrants or the thousands dead from COVID, but maybe losing his own children has sent him spiraling off the deep end. Loss can be so painful." She sighed, almost feeling sorry for him.

Kate watched the news, searching for answers. Reporters and anchors discussed the new normal with expert guests. "With no guns being used by law enforcement or the military, do you expect spikes in violence in other ways?" someone asked. The short answer from every expert panelist: "We don't know."

It almost seems like some in the media miss the violence, Kate thought with disgust.

"What does it mean? What will it mean? Will the world grow violent in other ways without guns? What about knives? Or fists? Will criminals feel cocky knowing the remaining cops aren't armed? Before the mass shooting, gun owners argued they needed to protect themselves from attacks and violence; really, they meant other people with guns, right?" Kate speculated out loud while watching the interview.

"Shush, let's hear what the experts say," Kyle replied.

"No one really knows what will happen, but we anticipate there will be spikes in crime. There has been some increase in petty theft but not violent crime. How long will this new norm last? We don't know," one expert repeated. "But what we do know is that without guns, murder rates across the country have plummeted."

"That is great news," Kate said.

Another analyst, a famous psychologist, added, "It is odd that with so much added stress and fear, violent crime everywhere has gone down. Often stress and fear increases crime. It plummeted at the beginning of the pandemic, but gun violence and other crime escalated as society opened in June. There is speculation that with so much loss and sadness in the world, people just don't want to add more. We are in unprecedented times. We need to collect data and do more interviews; there is still no logical explanation for the mass shooting. Even the conspiracy enthusiasts have calmed down. Maybe things, including violent crime, will not return to normal until we determine what caused the shootings on July 14."

The anchor wrapped up the interview to cut to a CDC official press conference. The official stated, "The mass shooting suicide victims have mostly been buried or cremated by now. This is great progress for public health and mental health as it allows our nation to mourn. Unfortunately, COVID cases increased temporarily. The shooting caused people to get too close to each other when dealing with the deceased, often not wearing masks when attending funerals and mourning with loved ones. It's understandable; we were all panicked. This caused cases to spike for several weeks. We are also noticing that in the past few days, people are back to washing hands, socially distancing, and wearing masks when outside. We appreciate everyone working together to keep each other safe. We have all lost too much; we don't want to lose more."

"I feel bad saying this, but with so many people dead, even with that spike in cases, I doubt the hospitals are as slammed as before the shooting. Can't be," Kyle said, clicking off the TV. "Come on, babe. Let's get some fresh air. Sit outside."

They moved away from the TV, taking their beverages to the front porch.

"Covid is up, then down. Violence is up, then down. We need more data, more expert opinions," Kyle said with a loud sigh. "Just kidding. Hell, I don't think anyone really knows anything. Even if we get more data, the baseline will just flip over again," Kyle said. "And no one wants to say it, but maybe gun owners were generally more violent people."

"I think gun owners were more scared and thought guns would bring them more control. I think people are realizing they are not in charge. It's not about personal freedom. There are things, energy, powers, bigger than us calling the shots, literally," Kate said, the image of Rex crossing her mind.

"We should stick together more. We need to stick together. Help each other out. Stop fighting over everything. Even the Republicans in Congress have stopped telling everyone it's 'us against them' regarding masks. At least for now," Kate rambled on to Kyle as she watched squirrels run around outside.

Kate was drinking wine and Kyle beer.

"What day is it?" Kyle asked.

"Tuesday," Kate replied.

Kate smiled; this was a running pandemic joke. The days ran together, but no one complained of boredom anymore. Everyone would take endless boring days over a mass shooting.

"It's strange how we all say 'mass shooting.' It was a mass suicide. Someone on the news was saying we should correct our terminology," Kate said.

"Why? Are we offending mass shooters?" Kyle joked. "Also, mass suicide doesn't seem fair. I doubt all those people wanted to kill themselves."

Suddenly, a car pulled up in front of their house and four people got out. Kyle and Kate watched this rare event on their quiet street with curiosity, sipping their beverages.

But when the strangers started to walk into their small yard and toward their steps, Kate went from curiosity to alarm.

"Hi Kate, I am Tonya, and this is Robert, Malcolm, and Jo-Ellen. We are with Space Force. We need to talk to you, please," a woman with a tight bun on top of her head said, sliding her sunglasses down to make eye contact with Kate as she walked to the bottom step.

Kate slipped her mask back over her face.

The Space Force employees responded similarly, reaching into pockets for their masks. Kate was annoyed that they had been in the car together without masks on. *No wonder this virus keeps spreading.*

"Can we come inside?" Tonya asked.

"Absolutely not," Kate replied. "We're in a pandemic. Our closest friends haven't been in our house for months."

"Oh, don't worry. We get tested regularly. We're deemed essential, and our job requires us to engage with people," Tonya explained.

"Well, we aren't," Kate replied, glancing at Kyle. She could tell by his face he was willing to invite them in, but Kate shut him down with a look. "We can talk out here. What is this about?" Kate asked Tonya, standing up from her sitting position on the step. Her heart was beating fast, but she tried to keep her breathing calm.

"A couple weeks ago, you sent an email to Carol Simmon, your supervisor, about an incident you had in Rock Creek Park. Someone in the park claimed responsibility for the mass shooting? Told you more violence was coming? Is that right?" Tonya asked.

"Ah no, that is not entirely right," Kate responded nervously. "I mean, I made the assumption it was about the mass shooting. They never said the words 'mass shooting,' and they didn't take direct responsibility for what happened. They just suggested there would be more violence."

"They?" Tonya asked. "There was more than one?"

"No, just one," Kate said.

"Okay," Tonya said with a sigh. She pulled a phone out of her pocket and started to type. "I have a few specific questions. Please answer accurately. Malcolm will write down exactly what you say, and I will also be taking some notes. Would it be okay if he sits on your step? Easier to hear you and write."

I've been so focused on watching for Rex's actions and worrying about the threatened violence that I forgot to be worried about Space Force. And I was more concerned Carol would write me up for mental stress or something, not actually report my harasser's warning. I want to kick myself for putting it in writing. I even told Sinclair to talk to a friend at NASA, knowing that putting things in writing causes problems. Then did it to myself at Space Force. Obviously, I never learn.

Kate nodded yes to Tonya.

"Okay, sure, shoot," Kate winced at her inappropriate expression. She was nervous. Did she need a lawyer? Surely not. She quickly decided she would just answer their questions simply and honestly but not offer anything extra.

"Great," Tonya replied. "What day did the encounter occur?"

Shoot, Kate thought. There were two encounters, but she never made that clear to anyone. She decided to focus on the second. Everything important happened in the second engagement. "I can't remember the exact day. Hold on," Kate said, getting out her phone. She focused on July 14, the day of the shooting, and counted to the first encounter. Then counted out the days to the second incident. "Sorry, but the days are a blur. They have been since mid-March, and the shooting has just made things so much worse."

Tonya tapped her phone impatiently, glancing at her colleagues as Kate looked at her calendar. "Not very memorable if you can't remember the date of the incident. What about day of the week? Any recollection of that?" Tonya asked a bit sarcastically.

Kate's cheeks grew red and her heart was racing, but then she took a deep breath and slowed down. Let them think she made it up or exaggerated—fine by her.

"Now let me see. What day was the shooting? Right, July 14. That was a Tuesday," Kate said looking at Tonya and the others as if for confirmation. "It's like before the mass shooting and after the mass shooting for us all now. Really life changing." Kate nodded at everyone as she continued to delay.

Tonya sighed loudly and stuck her hip out in a gesture of annoyance but said nothing.

"Okay, Sunday, August 2. I went for a run, and that is when it happened," Kate stated confidently.

"What time?" Tonya snapped.

"Early. I was trying to beat the heat," Kate said, knowing it would not be good enough.

"Is that 5 a.m., 6 a.m., 7 a.m., or 8 a.m.? What do you consider early?" Tonya asked.

"Around 8 a.m. My definition of early has really slipped since March. Is that the same for you all?

Maybe not since you don't work from home. We work from home, so without a commute or coffee runs, we sleep later. Right Kyle?" Kate said, gesturing to Kyle.

Kate realized her mistake, bringing the attention to Kyle, when Tonya immediately looked at Kyle and started to ask him questions.

"You're Kyle Sullivan? You both live here? Together? Is that correct?" Tonya asked.

"Yes," Kyle responded. Kyle seemed startled to suddenly be addressed by Tonya.

"Do you remember when it happened, Kyle?" Tonya asked him.

"Yes. She came in and was upset and told me what happened on her run," he replied. "She said a guy scared and harassed her on her run and said something about more violence coming if she didn't warn people. Or something like that. Best to ask Kate, since she is right here and it happened to her," Kyle added. "Is this some kind of sexism bullshit? Because you should write down in your notes that I'm a feminist." Kate could hear the testiness in his voice.

Tonya cocked her head and looked at him quizzically. Kate smiled and loved him even more.

"Exactly where did it happen, Kate?" Tonya snapped to Kate.

"On a trail in Rock Creek Park," Kate snapped back.

"Exactly what trail and at what point on the trail?" Tonya asked.

Kate took another deep breath and decided to change tactics. She had no reason to be so agitated by Tonya and her team. They were just doing their jobs.

And what exactly are their jobs?

She smiled at Tonya and the others with her eyes.

"I'm a bit confused. What division of Space Force do you work for? Why is Space Force so concerned about some crank pot that it sent four people to talk to me? I mean, sure he was unnerving during these scary times, but this seems strange, maybe overkill. Has Space Force had other complaints? Are you, or Space Force, taking this seriously for a particular reason?" Kate asked, keeping her tone pleasant.

"Look, people are hyper-concerned that there has been no plausible explanation for the mass shooting. The government has been asked to chase down every possible lead, no matter how ridiculous. We're enforcement agents, but mostly analysts, indoor people you might say. We're new to the field. We're not armed, for obvious reasons, so they send us together for safety. We're all learning new skills in these trying times," Tonya explained.

Kate's paranoia washed away. These people were concerned Americans, just like she and Kyle were. *We're all on the same team.* "Of course, that totally makes sense. I hadn't considered the new world. I almost asked you if I should get a lawyer, like in the movies!" Kate added, smiling.

Two of the agents laughed, dissolving some of the tension.

Tonya continued to ask questions. "Where exactly did the encounter happen?"

"Off the Parkwood parking lot. There's a trail head running north, toward the Maryland border. Just a half mile up on the trail, max, maybe less," Kate said, wondering if they checked it out, if they would end up in the white room with Rex.

"Did anyone else see the interaction?" Tonya continued.

"Not that I know of," Kate replied.

"What were his exact words?" Tonya's interrogation continued.

"It's very important. You need to tell your leaders at Space Force that this was a warning. More violence will come," Kate replied, leaving out the deadline.

Kate thought the addition of the deadline was because she ignored the first warning from Obama, kind of added pressure for her slacking after the first encounter. There was no real reason to mention it now. Plus, the deadline had passed anyway. Obviously, her email to Carol had worked. There had been no more violence and it triggered a response from Space Force.

This is actually progress. Space Force is taking over, and I can get back to worrying about spreadsheets, not mass global violence, Kate thought, feeling relieved.

"It was a man who issued this warning, right?" Tonya continued.

Kate's stomach twisted in pain. Lying physically hurt. "Ah, yes, I think so."

"What? Yes or no to male?" Tonya asked.

"Sort of tall like a man. Sounded like a male. It was kind of confusing," Kate replied.

"Oh, like a non-binary or transgender identity?" Tonya said, nodding her head.

"Maybe?" Kate said.

Tonya moved on. "Did he say his name?"

"No."

"Did he have an accent?" Tonya continued.

"No."

"Did he mention any organizations? Maybe that he represented?"

"Nope," Kate answered confidentially, happy to not be lying.

"Did he mention any nations or countries or America?" Tonya continued.

"Nope." Kate shook her head.

"A political party or religion?" Tonya continued.

"No, and I would have said so if he had. He only said what I said. 'More violence is coming. Warn your leaders,'" Kate said. *How many times do I have to repeat the message?*

"Why Space Force?" Tonya asked.

"Don't know," Kate replied. "I didn't ask."

"Did he touch you?" Tonya asked next.

"No," Kate answered.

"Did you lose anyone in the mass shooting?" Tonya asked.

The change of course confused Kate for a second.

"Ah, no, not directly. Kyle and I were very lucky. We do know people who did though," Kate said. "It's such a tragedy."

"Have you ever owned a gun?" Tonya asked.

"No."

"Do you come from a family that had guns?" Tonya asked.

It was a strange question. "Obviously not, since we did not lose anyone in the mass shooting," Kate responded. Even before the incident in Colorado, she and her mom hated guns.

"What about COVID?" Tonya asked. "Have you lost anyone in the pandemic?"

"Not really. We have loved ones that lost loved ones but not us," Kate replied.

Are these Space Force agents trying to make me feel bad about being lucky I haven't lost anyone to either tragedy? Or maybe trying to determine my mental health state?

Tonya was typing hard into her phone. Malcolm was furiously writing. Kate took a big sip of wine, hoping they would think she had a drinking problem. Common condition during the pandemic and better than being insane.

"I think we're done here for now," Tonya said, sliding her phone into her pocket. "What about you, Malcolm? Ready for Kate to read and sign?"

"I have a question," Jo-Ellen said, speaking for the first time. "What exactly did he/she look like?"

All eyes were on Kate again.

Kate felt the pain again. She really hated to lie. "I don't know. It happened so fast. He jumped in front of me out of nowhere. I came to a screeching stop, and he told me more violence was coming if I did not warn my leaders at Space Force. He may have been white. He may have had orange-red hair. He may have been wearing cat ears, like a costume. I don't know. It was strange, and it happened very fast. I did what he said, and there has not been more violence. I feel I did my civic duty, and all is well that ends well. I've answered all your questions. I'm going to end this conversation now. Thank you for your public service," Kate said quickly as she rushed into the house and slammed the door before anyone could say another word.

When inside, she ran up the stairs to her bedroom and shut the door hard.

There's no way I'm going to sign that statement.

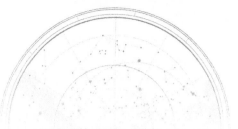

TWENTY-FOUR

Forty-Two Days After the Shooting

Another week went by, and Kate miraculously focused solely on work and volunteer activities. No death clocks. No Rex nightmares. No knocking on Sinclair's door.

Her boss, Carol, sent an email to Kate thanking her for helping the Space Force agents. "I heard the interview went well," she wrote.

Kate was eager to speak to Carol. She wanted to ask Carol who she told at Space Force. Kate wanted to know what in her email triggered such a serious response, sending four agents to her house. Kate wanted to know who saw her email and made the decision to send agents, but she didn't dare put those questions in writing.

Carol had been cancelling staff calls and one-on-one check-ins due to personal issues, but at this point, Kate had a feeling Carol was just avoiding her.

Kyle thought the interview went well and did not think it was overkill at all. Though he did want follow-up. "Do you know if the agents found the harasser in the park? Did they even try?" Kyle would ask occasionally. "I bet the nutbag went after lots of people. Bet that's why Space Force sent investigators. Not sure they would have if it was just a one-time incident. What do you think, Kate?"

Kate would just nod or shrug.

Sinclair had stopped over as well with lots of questions. He saw all the people in their yard. Many neighbors had noticed. Since mid-March and the start of the pandemic, everyone knew everyone's business on the street, like who lived in each house and who worked from home. Four strangers hanging out in the yard definitely got attention.

Kate let Kyle answer Sinclair's questions.

"Kate, come and watch this," Kyle called. He was on his lunch break and eating in front of the TV. "The mayor is talking about guns." He turned up the volume as Kate turned her focus to the mayor, speaking from a podium outside her office.

"Everyone is interested in guns like never before in our city and across the nation. Whether you were a steadfast proponent of Second Amendment rights or a passionate advocate for gun control, we are where we are today because of the role guns played in our lives. Now, in the aftermath of tragedy, we must reevaluate our relationship with guns. This is not about political party or the Constitution; the paradigm has changed forever. As investigations continue with the hope of someday being able to explain why the horrific event happened, we should all be aware of certain facts. We also have to be aware that there are some questions we may never have answers to. In the absence of information, we must not fall into rabbit holes of conspiracies. Conspiracies exist because people are scared. Unfortunately, it is human nature that when we don't know why something happened, we tend to make up reasons and justifications to soothe our fear, pain, and loss." The mayor looked out over the crowd of reporters, slid her mask down, and took a sip of water from a bottle that read "taxation without representation."

"That is bold," Kate said. "Did she just debunk all religions in one sentence?"

"Shush. That is not what she meant," Kyle said, watching the TV.

"I know, but it is kind of what she just said. And look at our awesome city, D.C., serving as the role of our nation's capital for a change instead of just being insulted," Kate said, impressed this was being televised live on a national cable network.

"Shush," Kyle said again.

"Before the shooting, an estimated 4,000 D.C. residents possessed legal, concealed guns on our streets," the mayor said. "At least 2,300 illegal firearms were present, based on what law enforcement seized in 2019. With so many law enforcement agents and permitted citizens, there were almost 60,000 registered guns in D.C. at the time of the shooting. The D.C. government will continue to carefully collect them. The vast majority of residents do not want to be anywhere near a gun until the exact cause of the mass shooting is determined. This hesitation, and logical concern, included D.C. law enforcement and agency employees. However, as time passed and we still do not know what caused the July 14 tragedy, we have begun collecting the weapons. Please continue to call 311 and press extension two to report guns that need to collected or go online to DC.gov/guns. As we have said before, these can be guns in your home, place of work, in the streets or parks, or anywhere. Just record the details of the location. Perhaps take pictures that will be helpful in locating them. Please be patient. A professionally trained person will come as soon as possible to retrieve the weapon. We have already collected nearly 25,000 guns in the city, so we are making progress. With your help, we are making progress."

"Any questions?" the mayor asked the reporters.

One reporter shouted out: "There have been people who found guns on the streets and are bragging on social media that they aren't scared and will take any guns people don't want. Some are saying that when things calm down and are back to normal, they'll be the only people with guns, insinuating they would be safe or in control. How is your office responding to these citizens?"

The mayor sighed loudly before responding. "It's extremely sad and disappointing that a few people are exploiting this tragedy. But they need to know as soon as we remove the danger from our city, and the nation, by collecting the discarded and unwanted guns, and rebuild our police forces across the nation in accordance with community policing standards, we will find them, and they may be held liable for theft. And they better have legal licenses for any and all weapons in their possession. If a person could not own a gun, for whatever reason, before July 14, they can't own a gun now."

The mayor continued sternly, "Since the NRA and most gun advocates are no longer with us, there have been fewer people to flame irrational fear about guns or the lack of guns. Fearmongering and conspiracy theories are mostly falling on deaf ears. The press, for once, is keeping things in perspective, and I am truly grateful. Please do not report internet lies and tweets as though they are facts or common. Like the exaggerated reports of looting in July. Since the shooting, we have all been working together, with transparency and trust. As we look out for the welfare of ourselves, our families, friends, and neighbors these past weeks and stopped focusing on tweets and clicks, we have better served ourselves, city and nation. Let's keep it up. Let's continue to build mutual trust and help each other through these extremely difficult and heartbreaking times."

The mayor's eyes flashed with a fire Kate wasn't used to seeing. "And let's remember, more than 70 million Americans died from their own guns on July 14. And let's also remember 57 percent of Americans, more than 180 million people, were living safely in a house without a gun on July 14. Continue to share these absolute facts, especially when challenged by anyone claiming guns are safe. Until we know what the hell happened, they are not."

"And please know, there has been a decline in violence throughout the nation and in D.C. since the mass shooting. A plummet in violent crimes and a continued significant decline in overall violence. There was some looting in a few cities after the mass shooting, which was blown out of proportion. People were afraid of food and other shortages, but it has stopped. Nationwide, there has been a huge decline in violent crime. I know we are afraid in these strange and uncertain times, but let's keep that in mind."

With that, the mayor ended the press conference.

"Hear that, Rex," Kate mumbled to herself.

"She should run for President. She is doing a kickass job," Kyle said, going back to his lunch.

"She is awesome," Kate agreed. She wished Rex had pulled the mayor into the cold, white box instead of her.

The national anchor came back and noted, "In addition to D.C. efforts, the federal government is sending out people and robots to collect guns from streets, alleys, businesses, parks, and homes all over the country. There were almost 400 million guns in America on July 14, and we are trying to determine how many have been collected to date. Since America had more civilian owned guns than any other country, the mass shooting hit Americans hardest. We have a multitude of guns to collect."

"It's so sad. America had the most shootings and the highest COVID cases," Kate said.

"We're number one," Kyle said sarcastically. "So much winning."

"And what are they going to do with all those guns? Melt them down? I just envision huge piles of dangerous garbage. So much garbage and pollution everywhere," Kate said. "Could the metal be reused for parts for playgrounds or buildings? What about all the plastic? What can be done to keep it out of the oceans?"

Kate could feel her heart rate increase and her stress level rise as she thought about global warming, pollution, and the destruction of nature. She squeezed her eyes shut and saw images of the Amazon, Australia, and California on fire.

She started to wonder if Rex was even real. Maybe she did have some stress episode and it did not happen. That was actually the most rational and logical explanation.

TWENTY-FIVE

Forty-Three Days After
the Shooting

K ate woke up the next morning with a deep, melancholy heavy in her gut. She tried to meditate. She tried yoga. She considered painting some peace rocks but knew none would make her feel better.

"I have to run," Kate told Kyle. "Or I fear I'll fall into a depression and never crawl out."

"Okay. Just stay on the roads. Stay on roads with houses," Kyle said absentmindedly as he headed to the kitchen to make breakfast and coffee.

Of course, he didn't understand why going for a run was a huge deal to Kate. He didn't know about the white room.

Sure, some weirdo might startle her again with a cryptic warning, or a mass shooting type event could happen, or someone might cough on her without a mask. Kate knew Kyle thought that these were the worst that could happen. She laughed to herself while putting on her shoes and yelled down to Kyle, "I remember when having to find a bathroom or tripping on a rock were my worst running fears!"

Kyle didn't respond.

Kate ran quickly down the stairs and out the door before she changed her mind.

She ran down the street, heading to the park. She veered right, away from her usual wooded path, just before the trailhead and continued on the paved bike path. The bike path had less shade and was always busier than the trails.

She slammed hard into the back of a runner who had come out of nowhere and stopped short.

"Oh my God," Kate said, grabbing on the runner's back, trying to prevent them both from falling.

"Jeez! Sorry, you came out of nowhere!" Kate was startled but not scared. This was a fellow runner, not Rex or Obama or a creepy made-up composite of them.

Kate laughed as she pulled out an earbud. "Wow, please be careful. There are collisions on these trails and paths all the time. You should just pull over completely before you stop and look both ways before you start. Share the sidewalk," she said loudly to be heard through her mask, while moving around the runner to start again.

She was inserting the earbud when a second runner blocked her path.

She looked up at his face and then looked again at the first runner, who had also stepped in front of her. They were blocking her.

"Hi Kate. Remember us? Jo-Ellen and Malcolm? From last week?" the first runner said. "We're with Space Force."

Kate pulled both earbuds out. "Yes. What are you doing here?" Her stomach got butterflies. *What was happening?*

"We both live nearby and run around here. Since your complaint, we've been keeping our eye out for your harasser," Jo-Ellen explained.

"Cool we ran into you," Malcolm added. "You can take us to exactly where the incident happened."

Kate shivered with the feeling this was not a coincidence at all; they had been watching her house, her movements.

"Okay, sure. Back this way," Kate said, turning back to the fork and the trailhead. "Wow, you all are taking this really seriously."

Jo-Ellen chuckled. "Not us. We think it's ridiculous. Space Force is taking it seriously, though."

Malcolm shot Jo-Ellen a look. Jo-Ellen just shrugged like she did not care what he or Kate thought.

As they approached the trail into the woods, Kate asked, "Why is Space Force taking this so seriously?"

"I don't know. They don't tell us anything. They're all: 'Watch her and find out where the incident happened but don't let her know.' Well, now you know. You know what we know, which is not much. Malcolm and I are computer analysts and coders. We're new to the field. I never wanted field work. Hell, I didn't want to work for Space Force. Now we spend our days sweltering in the August heat waiting for you to come outside. Sometimes, with the boredom and the heat and the running and the mosquitos, I wish I had been a gun owner," Jo-Ellen said.

Kate stopped dead in her tracks, processing Jo-Ellen's dark statement.

"Why are we stopping?" Malcolm asked.

"Because we're here. Right around here. This is where it happened," Kate replied.

Kate hadn't intended to take them to the spot, but it seemed like they just came up on it.

She hoped one of them would get pulled into the white box room. Rex would have his Space Force leaders, and Space Force would have the harasser. Kate could go back to running the trails. Everyone would be happy.

"Why the smile?" Jo-Ellen asked. "I figured this place bothered you, seeing how you haven't been out here for some time."

"I'm just happy you're here. I'm happy Space Force is taking this seriously. I'm happy you can tell your leadership at Space Force that you're investigating thoroughly and will get to the bottom of this soon. I really appreciate your coming out here," Kate said.

She hoped Rex was listening.

TWENTY-SIX

Forty-Three Days After the Shooting

Kate continued her run. She ran to the end of her favorite trail, parallel to the creek. She was feeling so good, she tacked on another mile. She'd done her civic duty. Space Force was taking the threat seriously. Even if she saw Rex again, either for real or in her head, there was no way he could accuse her of not trying. She was confident that Malcolm and Jo-Ellen were heading back to their home office to write a report and put this field work behind them.

One of her favorite songs came on, and she was dancing as she ran when she realized where she was.

The feeling hit super hard, almost like she was hit on the head.

The punch disoriented her but wasn't exactly painful.

Her stomach jumped into her mouth, and she came to an abrupt stop. She tried to spit to stop the horrible waves of nausea.

The white room.

Not again.

She sat down on the floor, gasping for air. She tried to put her head between her knees to stop the gagging.

The cold hit her like a wave and seemed to help with the nausea.

Once she could breathe, she wrapped her arms around her knees and looked around.

"Hello, Kate," Rex said from across the room in his slow way.

This time she paid more attention to details as she inhaled deeply.

He had a deep, male voice. He was probably male.

She decided to not be helpful because she didn't want to be here, feeling like this. She spent a couple of minutes just breathing and rubbing her arms and legs for warmth

"Hello Rex," Kate finally replied, slowly, just like him. After several more minutes, she cracked and asked, "Why am I here? I did what you asked." She was shivering cold, but expected it to warm up soon, like it had before. "Well?" she snapped when she got no response.

"Because you did what I asked," Rex finally replied.

Kate put her head on her knees and shut her eyes. "God damn it," she swore quietly. "You totally suck. Now you're making me swear and insult you, but you suck," Kate said, her eyes still shut.

She hated the expression "No good deed goes unpunished."

"You threatened me. That is why I did it," Kate responded angrily.

After several minutes, Rex replied, "No, I threatened Space Force, not you. You carried that message for me. Thank you."

Kate was warming up from both the room temperature increase and her anger.

"What do you want now? Space Force got the message. By the way, they've been watching me. They made me bring them to the spot on the trail where you grabbed me," Kate explained. "Why don't you take them? They can help you more."

Kate was not sure how much he actually knew. *Can Rex see what is going on in the real world?* "You should have grabbed them, Space Force staff. Cut out the middle-man, I mean, woman."

"You're also Space Force," Rex replied very slowly.

"No, you wanted Space Force leadership. You specified 'leaders who go into space.' I'm a budget analyst, as far from leadership as possible. And Space Force is new and doesn't go into space yet. That's still all NASA." Kate was pissed. She forgot her plan to not contribute anything.

She was so upset, she jumped up and paced a bit, still fearful there was not really floor under her. It was hard to see the floor and walls; it was all so bright and white and disorienting.

Rex started changing forms.

Different people she didn't know, an orangutan, a tree, Kate's mother, which caused her heart to speed up quickly.

"What are you doing?" Kate stuttered.

He became Rex again.

"I don't understand what you're doing, but I like Rex best, okay?" Kate said.

"You have to go and tell the leaders at Space Force to clean up the pollution. The garbage that is dangerous. If they don't, there will be more violence."

"Wait a minute," Kate snapped. "You caused all that dangerous pollution, all those gun piles. Mountains of deadly plastic and metal and lead. You must have caused the mass shooting. Who else? How? Why? It's your fault." Kate shouted questions and blame at Rex, pacing around in small circles while waiting for a response.

"I caused the violence. I did not cause the pollution. That was already there, everywhere," Rex finally said. "You must tell Space Force leaders, who go into space, they must clean up the dangerous pollution now. They must start immediately or there will be more violence. There *are* more weapons," Rex added.

Everything started to shake again but then abruptly stopped.

"You are brave, Kate," Rex added slowly. He flicked his tail a couple of times, seeming even more like a regular cat, if a cat was six feet tall and could talk.

This change in conversation confused Kate. She didn't know what to say.

"You have five days," Rex added as the floor shook.

Kate fell through a hole and landed in a superhero pose on the trail, this time gently.

"At least this part is getting better," Kate said, standing up.

TWENTY-SEVEN

Forty-Three Days After the Shooting

Kate sprinted home. She needed to write down every word she could remember before she forgot. "More weapons" kept going through her brain. *Sure, America and the world have more weapons. There are so many weapons in the world: knives, grenades, blow torches, bombs, nuclear bombs. What does Rex mean?*

Kate opened her computer and started typing before she even sat down.

WEDNESDAY, AUGUST 26, 2020 TRAIL RUN

- Tell Space Force to clean up the pollution
- The dangerous garbage
- If they don't start clean up immediately, there will be more violence
- He does not think he created gun pollution

- Must tell Space Force leaders, <u>who go into space,</u> to clean-up now
- There are more weapons

Five days to pass on the message

Kate paced around, replaying the conversation over in her mind. "Rex is a cat of few words," Kate said out loud, leaning over the chair and staring at her screen. "I think I got it," Kate said, relieved. "Oh wait." She added one more bullet to her list.

- I am brave

"Got what?" Kyle said, looking over Kate's shoulder.

Kate jumped back, and their heads accidentally banged against each other. "Damn!" Kate exclaimed. "You scared me!"

"Same here!" Kyle said, rubbing his chin where her skull had jerked back and cracked it hard.

"Who were you talking to? Who said you were brave?" Kyle asked. "Did you see the freak in the park again? I thought I told you to run the streets, not the trail." Kyle was now looking at her computer screen. "What's going on, Kate?"

"I honestly don't know," Kate said, slamming her computer closed. "I need to think. I need to take a shower. And I'm late. I actually need to get to work."

She did need to do all those things, but she also wanted to distract Kyle. "Later, babe, I promise, I'll explain everything." She quickly got in the shower, letting the warm water flow over her sensitive skin.

Afterward, she fussed in the bathroom, putting on make-up and blow-drying her hair, steps she had mostly given up since working from home.

She practiced various conversations in her mind, explaining to Kyle and her boss and the agents from Space Force about what she saw and heard. She practiced describing Rex and the feelings when she moved into and out of the white room. She tried it with just the facts. She pictured them telling her she needed help. She would be put on administrative leave. She was hopeful they would leave her in Kyle's care. She envisioned their kindness as they explained to her that her mental breakdown was clearly caused by the pandemic and shooting.

I will officially have a pre-existing condition, a mental health pre-existing condition, and will never afford health insurance again if I lose my job. When I lose my job.

She took a deep breath and decided to settle on a positive image. She would tell the truth and hope they believed her. *Why would I lie? We live in crazy times; anything is possible. Why would this not be true as well?*

She would take a day or two. Tell everyone on Saturday or Sunday. She had five days to stop the violence.

TWENTY-EIGHT

Forty-Three Days After the Shooting

Kate worked for several hours straight, her eyes burning from staring intensely at the screen. She was afraid if she peeled her eyes from the computer for even one minute, Kyle would sense it and start asking questions. As it was, she had to wave him off several times.

"Let's talk tonight," she mouthed the last time Kyle wandered over to her while she pretended to be intensely focused on her work.

Kyle held up six fingers. "Front porch. 6 p.m. sharp. I will have adult beverages waiting. And I want the whole story."

Kate threw herself into her work so hard that she did not realize it was after six. Finally, she stood up and stretched. She walked slowly down the stairs. She had been working in the bedroom all day, which was unusual. She did it to avoid Kyle. She still didn't know what to tell him. He'd seen her post-run list, but how much had he absorbed? Earlier, she had practiced telling him the entire truth, but now that seemed impossible. She opened the front door, and Kyle jumped up. He'd been sitting on the top step.

"Hi, babe!" Kyle said, with arms wide open for her to go in for a hug. He had a beer in one hand, a wine glass in the other. "Let's go! Happy hour hug!"

Kate squeezed his torso and smiled, taking the wine he offered. She was feeling better already.

After they sat down, with Kate leaning on Kyle, he jumped in. "What happened on your run today, Kate?"

Kate took a deep breath, a slow sip, and took Kyle's hand. "I can't say. I can't tell you yet. I need to think. I'll tell you when I'm ready, maybe by Sunday," Kate said. She figured she had until sometime Monday for Rex's deadline. "Definitely by Monday."

She took a sip of wine. She knew she sounded strange, but she really did not want to lie.

Kyle looked at Kate, brows knit with concerned. "Okay, when you're ready to talk, I'm here to listen and help in any way I can."

Kate was surprised by his mellow, supportive acceptance of her decision not to share anything yet. She smiled at him, relieved.

"I think we should have another fun, long relaxing weekend. Let's take tomorrow and Friday off. It's the last week in August during a pandemic in a post mass shooting world. Who will care? You should take a bubble bath or two. We can make guacamole. We should watch more comedies. Another no stress weekend. A mini-staycation," Kyle added.

He thinks I'm losing it.

He saw the list. He did not hear anything about Rex or any details, and he is protecting my mental health, treating me like I am having a breakdown of some sort, Kate thought. She'd made the right decision to say nothing yet. If she had told him everything about Rex, he might insist on taking her to a hospital.

They sat on the porch for a while, drinking, talking, and occasionally laughing, only moving inside when mosquitoes got too obnoxious. They watched a movie and drank more wine. Kyle went to bed around midnight, but Kate could not shut down her mind. She went back on the front porch and listened to the summer night sounds, insects, the occasional car, and dogs barking. She was drinking a large glass of water, trying to counter the buzz she had from drinking wine for hours.

She heard Sinclair's front door open and close. She saw him walk across the street, put on a mask, and enter her walkway to their porch.

"Hi Kate," he said, standing six feet away. "How are you doing?"

"Fine. How about you, Sinclair?" Kate asked.

"Good. May I sit?" he asked.

"Sure," Kate gestured.

Sinclair sat down on the bottom step, and Kate slid back to the middle of the porch, ensuring they were six feet separated.

"You spoke to Space Force agents again today?" Sinclair asked.

Kate had just taken a large gulp of water which came out her nose and she coughed, reminding her she had come out without a mask. "Shoot, sorry!" Kate said. "Let me get a mask."

"Don't worry, Kate. We're outside and far apart. What did you tell the Space Force agents?" Sinclair calmly asked.

"I ran into them on the trail running. They wanted to know where I was harassed by Rex. They wanted to know exactly where it happened. I showed them. No big deal," Kate said, taking another sip of water. "Why do you ask?"

"Remember how I told you I spoke to someone at NASA about your incident?" Sinclair asked.

"Yeah." Kate played it cool. She really had not given it much thought since she told Carol and triggered the brouhaha with Space Force. "What happened? Who did you speak to?"

"I talked to an old friend. He trains astronauts. He has been with the agency for decades and is pretty tapped into everything NASA. He said he heard about your warning first from me and was mildly curious, but he thought the guy who harassed you was just a crackpot. But then he heard about the situation from another NASA employee. He did not tell anyone that he had previously heard the same story from me. He just listened," Sinclair explained.

Kate stared at Sinclair, nodding her head to encourage him to continue.

"He called me a couple of hours ago. He said he heard Space Force had a lead on what caused the mass shooting. He said Space Force enforcement staff specifically assigned to the mass shooting are saying they have 'a person of interest' and they are questioning that person," Sinclair said. "You might be the person of interest he heard about, Kate."

Kate shrugged and took a big gulp of water. "What difference does it make?" Kate's buzzed mind was trying to put it all together while not giving anything away at the same time.

"It could make a big difference going from reporting an incident to being the person they think made the threat or had something to do with the mass shooting. A big difference, Kate," Sinclair warned.

Kate was quiet for a minute. This couldn't be happening again. Her commitment to the truth, to doing the right thing, couldn't be coming back to hurt her again.

"Thanks, Sinclair, for letting me know. I really, really appreciate it," Kate said, heading into the house.

TWENTY-NINE

Forty-Seven Days After
the Shooting

By Sunday morning, Kate could not take all the relaxing and constant love and support from Kyle. She was not ill, mentally or physically, and his efforts were not helping.

She had played out every scenario involving Rex and Space Force that she could imagine and realized she needed to bounce it all off the one person who could give her solid advice.

She knocked on Sinclair's door.

He opened it fast.

"Hang on, I need a mask," Sinclair said.

"I'm coming in," Kate said, following him in the house. She walked straight through his house as she heard Sinclair rummaging for a mask. She opened the back door and stood looking over his little fenced city yard. *This is better*, she thought. *No one will bother us here.*

A minute later, Sinclair walked out in a mask. He handed Kate a cup of coffee.

Kate took the cup and stepped as far away from Sinclair as she could on the small porch to take down her mask. She took a sip of the coffee. It was good; she loved strong, black coffee.

"Did you have a dog?' Kate asked, looking at the small back yard. It had a nice patch of grass and boxes for flowers or vegetables or herbs, but they were empty and seemed liked they had been for some time. Nothing but dirt and soil. The strange thing was the wood fence. It was really high, at least seven feet, including the door into the yard. She had not noticed the fence was so high when she and Kyle were trying to get in to help Yvette the day after the shooting.

"No, not home enough. Well, until the pandemic," Sinclair responded.

Kate kept looking at the fence. It was distracting.

Sinclair must have noticed her staring. "Oh, you're wondering about the need for the privacy fence. Yvette and I have some expensive telescopes and equipment. We use it on the roof and back here sometime. It's best if no one knows."

Kate just nodded. It made sense to her. In this city, if something was not nailed down, it could be stolen. Telescopes would be very tempting. She took another slow sip of coffee, and still looking at the strangely tall fence, started to speak. "I'm going to tell you everything. Don't interrupt me until I'm finished. It's not a long story. You know strange things have been happening, not just to the world, but to me. I need to talk to someone who I think might be able to understand."

Sinclair nodded. He took the mask off one ear and took a sip of coffee, quickly replacing the mask. The movement made Kate notice for the first time that Sinclair was very handsome. His dark black face had a wide mouth and inquisitive, kind eyes. He wore his hair short and plain. He was taller than she was and very fit. She recalled how he rode his bike a lot and it showed. She figured she had not noticed how good-looking he was since he was older and married.

He's probably as close to forty as I am to thirty.

She took one more thoughtful look and then started to speak.

"On July 14, I was running in the park on a trail when the explosions started. I was scared shitless and ran home. Like most people, I didn't understand what happened until I saw it on the news. A few days later, I was running in the same place on the trail, and I was moved, snatched up. I don't know exactly how, but it felt awful, physically awful. I ended up in a white room, a freezing cold white room, speaking to something that looked like President Obama. It actually switched forms a few times. It was terrible, so scary. I think that time included the Pope and Kyle. Some kind of avatar, I think."

Sinclair's face remained expressionless. *Is that a good sign or a bad sign?* Either way, she'd started. She couldn't stop now.

"Anyway, whatever it was, it said, 'You need to do something. It's very important. You need to tell your leaders at Space Force that this was a warning. More violence will come,'" Kate recounted. It felt good to share the part about the person being able to change shapes.

Shape shifter? Is that what it's called in Sci-Fi movies?

"I decided to ignore the whole incident and go about my life. About two weeks later, it happened again at the same location and the same way. I know—why the hell did I go back, right? Well, I did," Kate said with a sigh. "That time, same warning, but with a deadline. I was given five days to issue the warning to Space Force. The exact message was: 'I will send you back. You have five days to tell your leaders this violence was just a warning and more is coming. I will know when you speak to them,'" Kate said in a different voice, trying to sound like Rex, like she was a school librarian reading slowly to a little kid.

Sinclair looked at Kate with a puzzled look, eyebrows pulled together, causing wrinkles on his forehead. But he also had a calm, encouraging manner, like he was trying to remail neutral and not judgmental.

After a minute of silence, Kate started again. She appreciated that he honored her request to hold all questions until she finished.

"Because of the deadline, I thought maybe I should talk to someone to cover my bases. At first, I really didn't want to bring this up with Space Force. As you know, Space Force is military. Space Force does not yet even go into space. NASA is space exploration. I mean, if my delusions were actually real, NASA would know what to do. Not the 'brass' at Space Force," Kate continued. She was concerned she was now talking too fast and confusing her thoughts and worries with the facts.

She paced the small yard, feeling anxious, reliving that day.

She took another sip of coffee.

"So, I spoke to you. You helped me solidify my idea that just speaking to people I knew at Space Force was enough to appease the request. And I thought just talking to you, a NASA scientist, would appease my concern. If, by some crazy long shot, the encounters were real and not in my mind, and Rex knew something about the mass shooting, then I had done my part by relaying the warning to the 'proper authorities.'" Kate paused again and stared at Sinclair.

This time he nodded and raised his eyebrows in a way to encourage Kate to continue.

"Wait, you aren't recording this, are you?" She glanced up and around the eaves of his house. "Do you have cameras?" Kate asked in a panic.

"No, Kate, the cameras are not on. I haven't turned them on since Yvette shot herself. I keep forgetting. And I'm not recording anything. My phone is in the house," Sinclair assured her.

"Okay, thanks. I should have asked before." Kate's voice trailed off, thinking about questions she had for him. She took a deep breath and decided to finish her story first, and then turn it around on him.

"After talking to you, I sent an email to Carol, my immediate supervisor at Space Force. She just manages a lot of analysts and contracts. I kept the email vague. I made it sound like the strange warning came from a random person in the park. I mean, technically that was true," Kate continued. "I was pretty stressed out until Friday, the fifth day, passed without incident." Kate paused for dramatic effect as well as another sip of coffee.

She felt a pressure lift off her chest. It felt good to talk, to share this with an intelligent, thoughtful person rather than just Kyle. She worried Kyle couldn't handle the whole truth.

"Once there was no additional violence that I knew of, I put the whole matter out of mind. But I avoided the trail and park, of course," she said. "Everything was calm until that Thursday evening when Space Force showed up at my house. I thought I had answered them completely and fine—fine enough for them to move on to important things. Then two agents jumped out at me on the trail Friday morning." Kate paused, wrestling with how to tell him about what happened after she saw the agents. About Rex's most recent message. If she told him, that was it. If Sinclair was just indulging her, he would now realize how crazy she was. One could say the virus and mass shooting triggered her first mental episode. Maybe the second as well, but a third meant she believed it all.

Mental evaluation here I come.

But then Kate decided she had to risk continuing. She had a five-day deadline before more violence might erupt. What could be worse than a worldwide mass suicide? She did not want to know.

Sinclair had lowered his mask again and was sipping his coffee, patiently waiting for Kate to resume talking.

More haltingly, Kate went on. "After I showed the agents where the incident occurred, I continued my run. I felt good, like the whole thing was over this time. I had done what I was told by Rex. Space Force actually thought it important enough to look into, even if the agents are disinterested and annoyed. Bonus that no one asked me for a psychological evaluation or my resignation. I thought, or hoped, it was over. So, I continued my run. Kept running on the trail and turned around after a few miles and headed for home."

Sinclair nodded slowly in encouragement to continue.

Okay, maybe he won't think I'm crazy.

"As soon as I got close to the location of the previous 'encounters' with Rex," Kate used air quotes and a facial expression to show how stupid she knew she was for going near that place yet again. "Swoosh, I was back in the white room, gagging on my stomach and gasping for air. Again."

His mouth twitched. *What does that mean? Does he believe me?*

"Rex gave me a new warning with a new five-day clock, which ends on Tuesday. This warning also included that Space Force needs to clean up the pollution. I have no idea what that means," Kate explained. "Because of your warning on Friday night, I decided I needed to tell you everything." Kate went to take another sip, but just the cold bit at the end remained.

"So, here I am. You and I are the only people on the planet who know everything," Kate said.

Sinclair didn't say anything. He just reached for Kate's empty coffee cup and walked inside.

When he came out, he handed Kate a full, hot cup. She took a few tiny sips, waiting.

When Sinclair finally spoke, he said quietly, "You haven't told me everything, Kate."

THIRTY

Forty-Seven Days After the Shooting

"No, that's it," Kate said. "I swear!"

"Who's Rex?" Sinclair asked.

"Oh, right. I don't know," Kate responded. She had not allowed herself to really think about this. She preferred to think of him as her "nutbag harasser" or a shapeshifting avatar rather than really think about what Rex was. She also knew Rex and the white room were the reasons other people would think she needed a psychological evaluation and mental health help; these were two huge concerns of hers regarding this whole experience. They put people away for less. Well, until the "you have other weapons" comment. That definitely sounded scary crazy.

"Frankly, I'm not sure," Kate said. "But maybe just us talking will avoid any problems again. And I can call Tonya to say he popped up again on the trail. I can do the bare minimum to avoid more violence. So far, so good. I don't really care who or what Rex is. I just want to be left alone."

Sinclair crossed his arms. "Not sure that will work again, Kate. Not that I know what Rex will do, but too many people are interested in your situation. Your email got around. It was forwarded to NASA and people on the space flight team. My friend got it and sent it to me. The rumors are that Space Force has a lead on figuring out what caused the mass shooting. They're kind of bragging, like I said, about a person of interest. I think they're being obnoxious. But it gives them credibility, having the first lead, and Space Force wants credibility." He paused, eyes gazing at Kate's face. "I'm relieved that what you told me tracks with what I saw in your email to Carol. That tells me you're being truthful. I appreciate that."

"It's scary, being a person of interest. I have honestly been worried about losing my job and/or mind and forced into taking a mental health leave of absence." Kate shrugged. "Though given this year, it probably wouldn't be the end of the world to take some time off." Who could blame her? 2020 was a total dick.

"I am sure they think you are having mental issues, Kate, but I fear they think you know more, or maybe even had something to do with the mass shooting. Anyone that was involved with the shooting of millions of people would have to be unstable. The level of violence is unprecedented and incomprehensible," Sinclair added.

"Right. Of course, it is. And also evidence I had nothing to do with it." Kate almost laughed. How could she have orchestrated such an event? Even if she had that kind of power, which she didn't, she'd never use it for bad. She wanted to save the earth, not destroy it. "I have no idea how it was coordinated or why. And I'm confident we can easily convince anyone that it was beyond my intelligence or imagination. That would be easy," Kate said. "I'm an analyst, for God's sake, not a terrorist."

"But you are the only person on Earth who knows the person claiming responsibility. Whether or not Rex actually did it, he's the only lead, and that's huge. All the governments in the world are rushing to find out what happened and why." He looked at her with solemn eyes. "They'll be coming for you soon, Kate."

"Space Force?" Kate asked, her cheeks burning hot.

"The federal government. Maybe Space Force will take the lead. I am sure they are trying to do so. It seems more an FBI or CIA thing. The shooting was worldwide, so the Department of Defense is probably involved, maybe saying it was an act of war. I don't know; I'm just speculating," Sinclair said.

"My primary concern has been with appeasing Rex to stop more violence, just in case he was being truthful. It has not been appeasing my government," Kate said.

"Rex chose you, I suppose, because you work at Space Force, but how did he know that? Was he following you? Did he google you? Maybe he works at Space Force too, and it's an inside job? What if he lives around here and knows your running schedule? Did you give a description of Rex to the Space Force agents? Did they do a composite drawing? Did they post it in the park?" Sinclair kept posing questions but didn't give Kate space to answer. "Maybe that should be your angle. The next agents or investigators who arrive from whatever agency, you get them focused on Rex. Yes, maybe you should say he popped up on the trail again. They need to find Rex and protect you."

Kate nodded her head enthusiastically. At first, she was trying to find a way to divert Sinclair from asking about Rex. Kate didn't want to talk about Rex. But Sinclair was just trying to help her not be the person of interest.

The person of interest is Rex.

"Makes sense. They should find Rex. He can answer all their questions. I certainly can't," Kate agreed. "Happy I didn't sign that statement I gave Tonya. I might have not given correct info on Rex."

"They are not the police or FBI, so I doubt that was an official statement. Could be an HR statement since you work there," Sinclair said.

They both jumped at someone pounding on the front door. It was so loud, the sound traveled through the house to the back porch.

"Stay here," Sinclair said as he went into the house.

A minute later he came back out. "It's Kyle. He's been looking for you. He seems concerned. I told him you were out back, and I would send you home."

"Okay, thanks," Kate said, heading in the door. She paused to put her coffee cup in the sink.

"I can't thank you enough. Just having you to talk to about all this has been extremely helpful. I'll do my best to make sure they get busy looking for Rex," Kate said.

Kate started walking to the front door.

"Hang on, Kate. You know what I do at NASA, right?" Sinclair asked.

"I know you're a PhD biophysicist. Your NASA bio says you do research, but it's written so vaguely that I am not exactly sure what you research. It does say you are well-educated, brilliant, and your research is vital to NASA's mission," Kate said with a smile.

"I study things brought back from space, mostly looking for carbon," Sinclair said, lifting one eyebrow as if he was sending her a signal.

"Carbon? You are looking for life? Extraterrestrials?" Kate said, goosebumps rising on her skin.

THIRTY-ONE

Forty-Seven Days After the Shooting

Kyle was on the front porch, hands on hips, red-faced angry when Kate ran across the street and up the steps.

"I'm so sorry. I had a quick question for Sinclair. I thought it would take a minute, but we got to talking and time flew by. Really sorry. I should have told you I was going out," Kate said in a gush to calm him down.

"Damn it, Kate. I was worried that freak came to the house or something. I even walked into the park to your trail head. I walked halfway to the hospital. Your phone was on the bed. I freaked out!" Kyle was almost yelling.

"I am really sorry, baby; I would have freaked if you just disappeared, too. It was inconsiderate. It was an accident. I had a question and thought it would take a minute, but Sinclair had an idea and offered coffee. Next thing you know, twenty minutes went by," Kate continued.

Kate hugged Kyle. It took a minute for him to relax and hug her back.

"It was forty minutes. I hope you didn't get COVID," he continued, pouting.

"We both had masks and talked outside. Kyle, we were safe," Kate soothed him.

He pulled out of the hug and asked, "What were you talking about, anyway?"

"About the freak harasser, of course. Sinclair had questions about the Space Force investigators. He said my email to Carol was leaked, and someone at NASA showed it to him. We were trying to figure out why. We have a theory. It's all worrisome. I need to think," Kate replied as they walked in the house.

She led him to the couch, and they both sat down. She rested her head on his shoulder, turning him to face the TV. "But not now. Let's relax. Who's playing?"

Kyle released the tension in his shoulders. "Okay. I may have overreacted. I was just worried," he said, looking at the TV. "The game just started."

Kate sat with him for several minutes watching. She seldom watched sports with Kyle, and her enthusiasm to do so now was a silent apology for making him worry.

Kate was relieved that he got lost in the game. She needed to process what Sinclair said.

As Kyle watched the game, she got up and found a notebook and pen and filled a water bottle with ice water.

Her hands were shaking. *Too much coffee or nerves?*

She paused briefly and stared at the TV, acting like she was interested in the game. She had no idea who was playing. She only knew it was European soccer, whereas Kyle was now completely engrossed, standing in front of the couch watching.

"I am going to sit out back and do some work, babe," Kate said. Kyle just nodded. His lack of interest in her and his hyper-interest in the game seemed like he was passive aggressively punishing her for making him worry. She headed out the back door.

She sat on the top step. Their backyard was much smaller than Sinclair's. It was just a little patch of grass and rocks with a chain link fence and little gate to the alley. You could easily jump the fence into the neighbor's yard and all the short chain link fences down the alley.

She was alone. No neighbors. No Kyle watching her attempt to draw a picture of Rex which she could convincingly tell government agents to look for.

It was interesting that Sinclair did not ask about the white room. Maybe he missed that part of her story. It was a lot to take in. Probably for the best, Kate thought, as she tried to remember exactly what she told the Space Force agents he looked like. Keeping the stories straight was getting complicated.

Did I actually say he was white with orange hair and cat ears? If so, I am an idiot. Or did I say he was wearing a costume? Maybe not a total idiot, Kate thought as she drew.

Just then, a huge wind hit Kate so hard that it pushed her stomach into her mouth. She was flying so fast; she could not breathe.

When she landed in the white room, she vomited up a mix of water and coffee.

THIRTY-TWO

Forty-Seven Days After the Shooting

K ate gasped for air. She backed away from the puke and sat down on the floor, wrapping her arms around her knees. By now, she knew it helped her adjust faster.

She was cold, feeling the shock of teleporting from sitting outside in August heat; literally going from 80 and humid to 30 and frigid in a split second.

As she calmed her breathing, the room temperate increased. After a couple minutes, she unwrapped her arms and looked up at Rex. She was angry.

Fuck this dude. Or cat. Or whatever he is.

"I was not on the trail. That's where you grab me! Not my back steps!" Kate shouted at him. "And it hasn't been five days yet! And I told NASA and was getting ready to communicate with Space Force! I was doing what you asked," she yelled. "By the way, if Kyle looks for me, and I'm gone again, he will freak out. I'm so sick of all of this shit! You can't just abduct people when they least expect it."

She knew shouting was not going to help. She did not have much of a temper, so even this outburst made her feel bad and tired.

The weird white walls and floor were giving her vertigo. She sat down and crossed her legs to ground herself.

"Why am I here?" she asked more calmly.

"We are running out of time," Rex said very slowly. "I told you—you have to tell the leaders at Space Force to clean up the pollution. The garbage that is dangerous. If they don't, there will be more violence. I told you I caused the violence; I did not cause the pollution. I told you Space Force leaders must clean up the dangerous pollution now. I told you that you had five days."

"I know. I was there. I mean here. I heard you. I told NASA and was going to tell Space Force soon. My five days is not up," Kate replied.

"Kate, you were right to involve NASA," Rex said, changing into Sinclair.

Kate was stunned into silence. She tried to pull it together, stuttering, "How, how, do you know Sinclair?"

"I see energy, Kate. I think that is the best way to explain it so you can understand," Rex/Sinclair said slowly.

"You see energy? No, that doesn't explain anything." Kate's head was spinning.

"When you move, talk, think, or feel, you are using energy. I see the energy," Rex/Sinclair added in his slow cadence. "But that does not matter. They're coming soon. They won't be as calm as I am. They'll be impatient to have it resolved and move on. We must move faster."

"Who's coming? Where are they coming from? Why are they coming? What will they do?" Kate said, jumping to her feet. This sounded ominous. She thought about all the bodies after the mass shooting, the chaos, and the "other weapons" comment from their last meeting.

"You need to tell Space Force and NASA everything I told you. You must be clear. Tell the leaders at Space Force and NASA to clean up the pollution, the dangerous garbage. They must do it now; if they don't, there will be more violence. They are running out of time," Rex/Sinclair said.

"What? They will think I am crazy! What pollution?" She was frustrated and had many questions. "I'm an analyst in the accounting department. I work with appropriations and program money. You need to understand how unimportant and far from leadership I am. They might arrest me. They might already consider me a *person of interest*."

She needed him to understand the gravity of the situation. Her career—her life—was at stake.

"We don't have time for this. Tell them what I said. They will understand. Tell them the deadline," Rex/Sinclair repeated.

"Do you even know what five days means?" Kate snapped.

Rex/Sinclair paused for a long time. "Yes, Kate, I do."

Sinclair shifted into Rex.

"They won't listen to me or believe me," Kate said petulantly.

"They already have," Rex said, turning into Tonya, the Space Force agent.

"Why would they believe me? This is big, huge, violent, scary and involves space. Why would they believe me, a nobody?" Kate asked.

"You are brave, Kate," it said, turning from Tonya into Rex. "And you know a biophysicist," he replied, turning back into Sinclair.

The ground shifted, and Kate landed pretty hard on her ass on her step.

THIRTY-THREE

Forty-Seven Days After
the Shooting

After Rex tossed her back into her own backyard, Kate rushed through her little yard, through the chain link fence gate, and made a beeline for Sinclair's, pounding on his door to the pace of her racing heart. He barely opened it a crack when she blurted, "We need to talk. More." She pushed past him and walked through the house to the backyard where she paced the length of his small porch, waiting for him to come out.

When he did, he was holding his laptop.

Kate just jumped in, talking fast. "I was just back in the white room with Rex. What the hell, right?"

"You went on the trail? Why?" Sinclair asked, forehead wrinkled in surprise.

"No. I was HOME, sitting on my back porch steps, writing notes as follow-up to our discussion. Getting my thoughts clear. I tried sketching a picture of Rex and then swoosh! I was back in the white room puking up coffee!" Kate explained. "Also, I planned to burn the paper after I wrote down my thoughts and pictures. I am not putting anything in an email or on a computer again. I'm not stupid."

"No, of course you're not stupid, Kate. Sorry, I didn't mean to upset you," Sinclair said. "I'm surprised Rex grabbed you at your house. That's new, right?"

"Yeah, and it's freaking scary. He can get me anywhere." Kate looked around, like Rex could be lurking in Sinclair's backyard. She wouldn't be safe until she did what she was told, even if it meant risking everything.

"We need to change our focus and thinking. Rex said we're out of time. That 'others' are coming and they will not be as patient. We need to forget about who or what Rex is and the white room. I need to stop worrying about my job or people thinking I am insane or fear of being a 'person of interest.' We need to focus on the dangerous pollution and get it cleaned up," Kate said, pacing. "The question is: what does he mean by 'dangerous pollution'? All pollution is dangerous. Plastics kill wildlife. Tiny plastic is in all our bodies and can cause cancer. Chemicals? Most are dangerous and pervasive. PCPBs are in the water. Coal ash? Lead? Pesticides? It's all poison. What about the enormous landfills all over the world? Or leaking toxins into our waters? Methane burning 24/7. What about the other greenhouse gasses?" Kate went on, growing agitated at all the ways humans were polluting the Earth. "God knows that it's all dangerous. No wonder so many people have cancer, not to mention autism, autoimmune diseases, and COVID."

"Great minds think alike," Sinclair said, showing Kate the laptop. "I've been focusing on the pollution comment since you left. Everything you listed is dangerous, of course, but this type might be of more interest to Rex."

She started reading the scientific paper on his screen. Kate realized they were standing right next to each other. Her fear of Rex and more violence trumped her fear of COVID. She sat down on the top step, putting the laptop on her lap. Sinclair sat down next to her.

The summary discussed pounds of metal, plastic, and other materials moving at extremely high speeds. It had temperatures and combustible figures. The article used the metric system and Celsius degrees, both of which always confused Kate.

"Sinclair, I am not exactly sure what I am reading," she admitted after a couple of minutes.

"Wait, this may help to clarify," Sinclair said as he typed on his laptop.

He pulled up a newspaper article from a few months ago.

Kate read parts out loud. "A dead Soviet satellite narrowly missed a Chinese rocket as it sped hundreds of miles above the Earth's surface, another in a series of close calls for junk whizzing around in orbit. In the space community, there is concern that objects will collide, creating massive debris fields and adding even more pollution to space that could last decades. Every collision could produce thousands of pieces of space debris. There are a couple thousand operational satellites, a lot of trash in space from spent satellites, old rocket boosters, and the pieces and junk from previous collisions and military maneuvers."

Kate paused and looked at Sinclair, who nodded for her to continue reading.

"The more junk in space, the greater the possibility of additional collisions, which in turn would produce even more debris, further exacerbating the problem. Dr. blah blah with MIT said near misses happen multiple times a week. Just this year, the International Space Station has had to maneuver four times to avoid a collision with debris. Over the next 10 years, more than 50,000 satellites could be launched, contributing to more debris. The Pentagon tracks about 22,000 pieces of debris larger than four inches, but scientists say there are nearly 1 million larger than half an inch. With all the debris floating around in orbit, there are estimates that there could be as many as 400 collisions and 17 million close calls over the next decade."

She stopped reading and looked at Sinclair.

"NASA has been worried about the Kessler Syndrome: A theory that the density of objects in low Earth orbit, or space pollution, increases the chances of collisions between objects, generating more pollution and litter, thus creating more collisions. NASA worries that too much debris in orbit may stop space activities completely, even the use of satellites, for decades, generations," Sinclair explained.

"This is horrible. I've heard about this; I just kind of forgot. And I didn't realize how much there was or how dangerous it has become. It doesn't get a lot of media or political attention," Kate said.

"No pollution gets the attention it deserves," Sinclair added.

"So, we've been focused on how it will impact our satellites and space industry, without considering the danger to others," Kate said. "Holy cow. It's a ticking time bomb in space. This has to be what Rex is talking about."

Suddenly, they saw a small tree branch slide through the fence door. The branch pushed up the latch, and the door swung open.

Kate and Sinclair jumped to their feet.

"What the hell," Sinclair said, standing in front of Kate in a protective gesture. "This is private property. I am politely telling you to get out now!" His voice was stern as he walked down the porch steps.

"Okay. Yes, sorry. I thought it best if I came in, rather than eavesdrop from the other side of your fence," a woman said. Her sunglasses and black mask covered most of her face, and she had a baseball cap on the top of her head.

She quickly walked in, closed the fence door, and turned around to face them, lifting up the sunglasses and pulling down her mask.

"Jo-Ellen?" Kate asked.

"Yes. Hi, Kate. Nice to meet you, Dr. Sinclair Jones. I am Jo-Ellen Marshall with Space Force," she said as she moved through the yard to meet him at the bottom step. "And I recommend you lower your voices."

THIRTY-FOUR

Forty-Seven Days After the Shooting

"This is private property. You still need to leave," Sinclair said.

Jo-Ellen didn't look like she had any intention of leaving. "Okay, it's been really easy following you, Kate. Generally, you stay home or come here. Occasionally, you run in the park. But what has been a pain in the ass was losing Malcolm. Once I did, I was perfectly happy to hang out today in the alley. And, boy, did I learn a lot," she boasted.

"Why are you losing Malcolm? I thought he was your partner." Kate was too curious to immediately back up Sinclair's order.

Jo-Ellen adjusted her cap. "Malcolm is really enjoying that he has talked to the only person of interest in the mass shooting. He's told everyone at Space Force, and I have no doubt, people at DOD, NASA, Capitol Hill, probably the White House. He's telling anyone that will listen. He's an idiot and doesn't realize what this can do to your life, Kate. What if everything you're saying is true? If Rex is real, we could be in danger of more mass violence. Last time it was guns; next time it could be nuclear warheads. However, if you are indeed delusional and there is no Rex, then Malcolm spreading your name around as the only person of interest on a mass shooting that killed tens of millions of people puts you in danger."

Jo-Ellen paused. Kate looked at Sinclair, who was nodding his head.

"The government will want a scapegoat. Our government needs a scapegoat, someone to blame. Our nation needs to move forward and heal. How can we if we don't know how or why or who did it? Maybe it was you, Kate, the only person in the world who has claimed to have some knowledge regarding the incident and thought the information important enough to take to management at Space Force."

Dread washed over Kate.

"May we sit? It's so hot," Jo-Ellen asked, sitting on the bottom step before Sinclair could invite her. "Even if our government supports your trash theory and accepts that Rex is real, Malcolm has still caused problems for you. Twitter trolls, stalkers, the conspiracy crowd—it's only a matter of time before they know your name. You know how scary that can be, right, Kate?"

Kate thought about Colorado and felt a strong wave of nausea. She knew what it was like to be called crazy and a liar.

"And I already thought 2020 sucked," Kate said with a shaky voice.

"To hell with Malcolm and you," Sinclair said to Jo-Ellen. "Just leave. Go back to snooping if you aren't going to be helpful. We're on a deadline, in case you missed that part."

"Wait, Sinclair, maybe she can be helpful," Kate said, touching his arm, hoping her instincts were right. She turned to face Jo-Ellen. "Please go and tell everyone at Space Force that if they don't clean up the pollution, the dangerous debris now, there will be more violence. I mean, cleaning it up will help humans, astronauts, and satellites; we all benefit from it, and it will stop Rex. Seems like a win-win to me."

Sinclair and Jo-Ellen stared at Kate. "Yes, I realize I may end up in jail or an institution or terrorized by dangerous trolls or stalkers. I get it. Seriously, I understand the consequences. But what else can I do? If I can stop another global act of violence, I have to try."

No one said anything. Kate took a deep breath. "Jo-Ellen, please carry this latest warning to Space Force leaders. Sinclair, please tell everyone at NASA. Either they take it seriously and try to save important and expensive equipment, future space exploration, and human lives, or they can be short-sighted, reckless, and selfish. Once they have the information, it's their choice whether to heed the warning. But I'm out. I'm so over being the intermediary."

THIRTY-FIVE

Forty-Seven Days After the Shooting

K ate ran across the street and into the house, slamming the door behind her.

"Damn, Kate, you startled me," Kyle said, glancing up from the TV. "Where did you go?"

"Sinclair's. Sorry, forgot to tell him something. Is the game still on? What sport?" she snapped. She did not mean to snap at him. None of this was his fault. She took a deep breath and realized it was still the soccer game. "Are you winning?" she asked more calmly.

"No, getting killed," Kyle responded. "Everything okay, babe?" he asked, taking his eyes off the TV and looking over his shoulder at Kate.

"All is well that ends well," Kate replied.

"Exactly! Seems Sinclair helped?" Kyle asked.

At least he seems over his earlier anger, Kate thought. "I have a headache. I think I'll take a nap," Kate said. She went upstairs and took a shower first. It was hot and she had been outside all morning sweating.

In the shower, she cried muffled sobs and fat tears. Kate was scared, frustrated, and angry.

"I feel like a sheep being taken to slaughter. I feel like a victim. I hate this feeling." She spoke to her reflection in the steam covered bathroom mirror.

It was just past noon, and she was mentally exhausted.

She laid down on the bed for a brief power nap that ended up lasting several hours.

The past merged with the present as Kate dreamt of blood and guns and mass shootings and Rex.

THIRTY-SIX

Forty-Seven Days After the Shooting

S he woke up disoriented.

What time is it? From the break between the curtains, it looked late. She pulled her phone from the bedside table. It was evening. How long had she been sleeping?

Her stomach growled. She heard Kyle's laugh coming from downstairs.

She got out of bed and changed her t-shirt and splashed cold water on her face, noticing sleep creases on her face.

She went downstairs and found Kyle on a web call with his family.

Kate was careful to stay off the camera. She held her finger to her lips so Kyle wouldn't acknowledge her. All she needed was his mom pointing out in her passive aggressive way how terrible she looked.

Kate made a quick salad and added a can of beans for protein. She grabbed one of Kyle's beers and headed to the living room.

The food made her feel better. She took a swig of beer.

Kate flicked on the news, and the beer shot out her nose.

There she was on CNN. The picture was from her Space Force ID card. It was not a good picture. Someone to her right had said something funny just as it was snapped, so her eyes were looking off and she had a ridiculous half smile.

"A person of interest has been identified in the massacre of July 14th," the anchor said.

Kate wiped the beer off her face with the back of her hand, whispering to herself, "Oh my God, oh my God," over and over.

Kate took another swig of beer. It might be her last.

"Kate Stellute is the first person of interest in the July 14 mass shooting. Stellute is an employee at Space Force and before that, NASA. That is all we know as of now, but we will follow this story very closely as it unfolds," the anchor added.

"Just like Jo-Ellen said, they're feeding the stalkers, trolls, and conspiracy crowd. It's over now," Kate exclaimed out loud. She raised her beer to the ceiling and toasted to Rex. "Not sure what is happening, Rex, but I believe I may have failed you." Kate downed the rest of the beer.

"Who's Rex?" Kyle asked, walking in the living room.

"Look, I'm officially a news story," Kate said, intentionally distracting him from Rex.

"What the fuck!" Kyle exclaimed, seeing Kate's photo on the big screen TV.

Kate got up and went outside to the front porch. She sat on the top step and put her head in her lap, fighting back tears. She jumped when she heard a cough from the street.

"Kate, get ready. They're coming for you," Sinclair warned from his side of the street.

"Yes, I know," Kate said loud enough for Sinclair to hear. "Thanks Sinclair, for trying to help." She went back inside the house.

"What is going on, Kate?" Kyle demanded. "Why do they think you're a person of interest? Do they think you had something to do with the mass shooting? That is ridiculous, insane. You hate guns."

"I need to change and get ready. I think I'm about to be arrested," Kate said, sounding calm but feeling nervous. She brushed her teeth, changed her clothes, and tried to control her hair. She gave up and put it in a ponytail.

Mug shots are never attractive anyway.

She wondered what kind of make-up worked best in jail, picturing herself with raccoon eyes from crying or smeared lipstick from screaming from torture. She decided to go with moisturizer and little else.

"Kate," Kyle called upstairs. "There are several vehicles in front of the house. Looks like cops and reporters!"

Kate sighed and headed downstairs to face her doom.

THIRTY-SEVEN

Forty-Seven Days After the Shooting

Kate grabbed her license, phone, and a twenty-dollar bill from her purse and put it in her jeans pocket. In the kitchen, she picked up a small hand sanitizer and her mask that read "Vegan for Life." Finally, she grabbed a hoodie; she'd heard jail could be cold.

Kyle had closed the curtains but was peeking through the front window. "There are two cop cars, a couple of regular cars, and two TV station vans," he reported.

"Kyle, I'm going out there."

He turned. She read the shock on his face. "What? What do you mean?"

"I'm going to turn myself in, I guess. I don't want drama," Kate said, impressed with her calmness. "I'll call you as soon as I can. Be ready to come and get me. Bail might be high. I have no idea. But come and get me when I call."

Kyle pulled her into his arms, holding her tight. Her heart was beating so fast, she felt the rise and fall of her chest against his. She tried to pull away, but he held on. "How long do you think they'll keep you?"

"I have no idea. I've never been a person of interest in a global mass shooting before," Kate half joked, still in his embrace.

"Fuck, Kate. This is totally crazy. Tell them they have the wrong person! Why aren't they going for the person in the park? Maybe I can come? Maybe there's something I could say that would help matters," he said, voice shaking.

They walked out the front door together.

Tonya rushed up the path to greet them. "Hi, Kate. Hello, Kyle. I hope you are both well," she said, smiling.

"Not well at all. Kind of freaked out about all these cars parked in front of our house and all the people. We're still in a pandemic," Kyle snapped.

"I know," Tonya said. "I assure you that we're all healthy and will be masked-up," she said, looking at Kate and ignoring Kyle. "Sorry. Kate, we need you to come with us for a talk."

"I told you everything I know," Kate said, watching Malcolm and other men block the reporters and camera people from stepping on the path that led to the porch steps.

"Well, not everything. So, we need to talk more. Would you come to Space Force with us?" Tonya asked.

"Am I under arrest?" Kate asked.

"Not yet. Not now. But it might come to that," Tonya replied.

"Do I need a lawyer?" Kate felt like arguing, telling Tonya to get a warrant or something. Kate knew about the criminal justice system from when she lived in Colorado, and she had learned a lot recently due to her involvement with Black Lives Matter. She knew the justice system could be lazy and corrupt.

But what about Rex and the pollution and violence? I have to do something.

Kate put her hand to her forehead and sighed. "Okay, I'll go and answer the same questions again if it will make you happy." Her knees trembled as she walked down the steps.

Tonya blocked her path, and with her back to the reporters, she whispered to Kate, "Go back inside like you're getting something. Leave the door open. Go through the house and into the alley; get in a black SUV parked behind your yard. We'd all rather avoid the press. After a few minutes, I'll go back on the street and get in my car. Meet you at Space Force."

"Oh, shoot Kyle, I forgot my water bottle," Kate said, turning and going into the house.

Kyle followed her in.

"I mean, if I am not getting arrested, I'm taking a proper water bottle. This is no reason for single-use plastic," Kate said over her shoulder to Kyle as she walked into the kitchen. She chose a light blue bottle that read "Save the Oceans—Use Less Plastic" and filled it with filtered water.

"You're not being arrested?" Kyle asked, confused.

"I guess not. Not now, anyway. Tonya said to go out the back door to avoid the press. There's a black SUV out there waiting for me."

"Should I come?" Kyle asked. "This seems really strange."

"No, I think I will be okay," Kate said, giving him a quick hug and kiss. "But babe, do we know any lawyers? Just in case? Maybe call around. Have someone on deck?"

"You got it," Kyle said. "Text me. Tell me what's happening or if you need me."

"See you soon. I hope," she added, walking out the back door.

THIRTY-EIGHT

Forty-Seven Days After
the Shooting

Half an hour later, Kate was sitting at a large conference table. On the drive over, and while being escorted through Space Force to the room, she had time to think. Jo-Ellen must have told them what she overheard, and this was the reason she was being brought in.

The two men in the SUV had introduced themselves when she got in. The one driving was Robert. He had been at her house the night Tonya interviewed her. She had already forgotten the other one's name. Now they sat in chairs along the wall. Their positions showed they were not important enough to sit at the table.

Kate was trying to calculate six feet of distance around herself when Tonya walked in with an older man in full uniform, including a Space Force mask. They were talking quietly but stopped when they got to the table and sat down across from Kate.

"Hi Kate, I am Acting General Carlos White. It's nice to meet you. I would shake hands, but perhaps an elbow bump instead?" She was surprised this guy was alive; he looked like the type to have a gun collection. Kate leaned back in her seat, pushed the chair away from the table, and gave a head nod. She figured the table only provided four feet of distance.

"Tonya has filled me in somewhat," he continued, but he was interrupted as several more people walked in the room.

As people sat down, they introduced themselves quickly.

General Someone Acting Vice Chief of Space Operations, Lt. General Acting Chief Operations Officer, Maj. General Acting Chief Technology and Innovation Officer: it went on and on. Nine Space Force staff, including Tonya and Kate, sat at the table. A diverse group of younger and middle-aged people.

When Kate first started at Space Force, she studied the appointees and management, curious about their titles and specialties. Their official pictures hung throughout the building. It was a brand new agency and interesting to watch it be created. Most of the leadership was old white men in fancy uniforms. However, many of those upper management and appointees had owned guns. Kate had stopped looking at the official emails listing the names of the dead; it just made her too sad.

Every person at the table had introduced themselves as "acting." Kate wondered if they were qualified to do their jobs or were just the next one down the line that did not own a gun, or maybe were just not close to their gun on July 14.

Kate just nodded as they said their names and titles, making no effort to remember them.

The door opened quietly and Jo-Ellen entered the room. She went to the wall and joined the gentlemen sitting against it.

"I think we should all spread out. We are in a pandemic," Kate suggested, pushing her chair farther away from the table.

"We're all wearing masks. We'll be fine," said Acting General Someone.

Kate shrugged and pushed her chair farther from the table and people.

"As I was saying, Tonya filled us in somewhat, but we have more questions," the General said before Kate interrupted.

"What did Tonya say I said?" Kate asked.

"Why don't you tell us about Rex?" the General asked.

"What did Tonya tell you about Rex?" Kate asked.

"Being deliberately evasive is not helpful, Ms. Stellute. You might be in serious trouble. We need to find this Rex immediately. If he was involved with the mass shooting, we need to know. We need to know everything about the mass shooting right now, and you're the only link to Rex. We must find out how it happened, and why, to be sure it does not happen again." The General spoke and held himself like the kind of guy who was used to having staff jump at each word he uttered.

Another uniformed officer—*seriously, how did this guy not have a gun?* —leaned into the table and said, "What I want to know is: why you?"

Kate shrugged. She had the same question.

"I mean, if Rex caused this horrific, global bloodbath, he must be one brilliant and evil son of a bitch. How do you know him? Why is he working with you? You're a program analyst in contracting! It makes no sense!" Kate couldn't see his mouth, but based on his eyes, she could tell he was seething. "Unless that's not your real job."

What? Now they think my analyst job is a cover?

"None of this makes any sense," the General added. "Why don't you start with how you know Rex?"

Kate sighed. "I don't know Rex. I don't understand what he is. I don't know if he's brilliant or an evil SOB. I don't know who he is, where he came from, or how to find him. Against my will, I spoke to him, or actually, he spoke to me four times. He gave me a message to tell the leaders at Space Force, which I did." Kate explained.

"We have to find Rex, now," the other officer said. "How can we contact him?"

Kate shook her head and shrugged.

"If you don't tell us where he is or how we can find him, you might be obstructing justice, Ms. Stellute, and you'll be in very serious trouble," one of the other officers said.

"I don't even know his name. I just called him Rex in my mind," Kate added.

The pissed off officer slammed his fist down on the table, making it shake. "Jesus Christ, General, this is getting us nowhere fast. She's not making any sense. This Rex has to be a brilliant mastermind or know who actually is behind the massacre. Hundreds of millions of people died at the same time, and she is being coy? Millions of Americans are in pain, are scared, are demanding answers, and she is playing with words? And look at her. We read her employee record. It makes no sense that he would reach out to her as a messenger. Maybe she's, what, his girlfriend? That would make more sense than an accomplice."

Jo-Ellen chose that moment to lean forward and contribute to the discussion. She pulled her mask down to be heard. "Ladies and gentlemen, Kate is our only connection to the person who may have caused the mass shooting. Rex, or whatever his name is, chose Kate to communicate with and asked her to communicate with us. So, let's communicate." Jo-Ellen sat back calmly, giving Kate a small smile. "He chose you, Kate, because you are brave. Isn't that right?"

Kate had wondered why Rex had said that, and now she wondered how Jo-Ellen knew. She did not want to think about it, to open that Pandora's Box of stress and emotion, so she put the comment out of her mind.

Until now.

THIRTY-NINE

Colorado

People always talked about the sky being bright blue on 9/11. The opposite was true for the day that changed Kate's life.

It was a cold, grey morning. Kate was in seventh grade and had just gotten off the bus and was heading toward the main building of her middle school, wading through a crowd of kids. Lost in thought, with her gloved hands holding both straps of her backpack, her mind ran through her classes and assignments, trying to make sure she had what she needed, wondering if she needed to stop by her locker.

"Kate!" someone screamed.

She whipped around, startled out of her thoughts.

But the kid was not shouting for her.

Just as Kate realized he meant one of the million other Kates at her school, she tripped over someone's bag, coming down hard on the bulky mass. Overtaken by embarrassment, she quickly struggled to get up. "Oh, I am so sorry!" she said to no one, reaching behind the bag to get leverage to push herself up.

As she pushed up, she looked behind her and she saw it.

She had tripped on a bag holding a gun, a really big gun. Maybe more than one.

As she scrambled up, a boy jerked the bag away and pulled it across his chest.

She looked up into his eyes.

He was taller and skinny with shaggy blonde hair. She didn't know his name. She guessed he was not in her grade because he seemed older.

Her heart raced as she stared into his eyes. Neither said a word.

He walked around her like he was going to head into school.

Her heart beating fast, her hands clenched into fists, Kate stepped directly in front of him.

"Please don't," she whispered loudly. "Go home, please."

He ducked around her to pass, and she jumped in front of him again.

"Go home, turn around, cut school," Kate pleaded.

She put her hands on his puffy winter coat. "Seriously, please, go home," Kate tried again.

He moved to go around her, and she dropped to her knees, looking up into his eyes. "I'm begging you. Everything is going to be okay. Just go home. Please, please, please, please go home," she whispered loudly so he could hear.

"Get a room," an older boy shouted at them.

A few people looked at them and laughed.

"You have to pull it out, Theo. That's how it works," another boy shouted, and more kids laughed.

Kate tried to reach for his hands, but he jumped backward, his bag almost hitting Kate in the face.

"Get up," he snapped.

Kate stood up, still looking into his eyes.

He leaned over and whispered directly into her ear, "If you tell anyone about this, ever, I will kill you. And I will shoot your parents, all your family."

Kate turned her head and whispered in his ear, "Please don't do anything. Please go home. Everything will be okay. I won't tell anyone."

The kid stepped back and turned around, heading back to the chaos of the bus drop area and away from the school.

Kate started to shake, fighting back tears.

"Are you okay?" one of her friends asked. "Do you know Theo? What were you doing?"

"No. I don't know him. I tripped over his bag. I was just apologizing," she said, hoping beyond hope that he'd left, that he'd heeded her words.

"Weird. It looked weird," the friend said.

"Let's go in. I'm freezing," Kate said, rushing into school.

She tried everything to put it out of her mind, but twenty minutes into second period, she started to cry. Big hot tears dropped from her eyes onto her notebook, smearing the notes she was taking. The teacher saw her distress and came to kneel beside her. "Why don't you go to the front office and call your parents? I don't think you're feeling well today."

At the office, Kate tried to explain that she had a headache and felt sick. She could not stop the fat tears from rolling down her face. She was worried; what if he went home and killed someone or himself? Maybe he had just walked around the building and was right now in second period with his huge bag. How did he get past the metal detectors? Sometimes they didn't work; she knew that. Maybe he was shooting people at a store? Or on a street? Or planning to take out all the kids in the cafeteria at lunchtime.

More tears flowed.

What the hell was she doing waiting here when he could be out there hurting people? Kate jumped up. "I'm okay now. Think I'll head back to class," she said to the office manager as she rushed out. She ran full speed to a door far from the front office and burst through it, setting off an alarm. She ran as fast as she could the two miles to the elementary school where her mother taught third grade. Kate was sweating and panting when she arrived. She threw open the front door, setting off another alarm, and ran to her mother's classroom.

"Hey Mom, I need to speak to you please, now," Kate said, breathing hard, cheeks and lungs burning.

A security guard came running into the classroom.

"No worries, Officer Rosie. She's my daughter," Kate's mom said to the guard. "What on Earth, Kate?" Her mom ran a hand over Kate's sweaty, teary cheek. "Have you been crying?"

Kate nodded.

"Officer Rosie, would you stay here a minute and watch these students?"

"Mom, you need to come with me. We need to leave this school. We need to go somewhere safe and talk. Now. Just trust me," Kate said, tears starting to flow again.

They walked out of the school together and rushed to Kate's mom's car, a beat-up Prius.

"What on Earth is going on?" her mom asked, her voice getting higher like it did when she was really upset.

Kate quickly explained what happened.

"What? Are you sure, Kate? That is a serious accusation? Wait, a boy at your school has a gun? We have to call the police, now!" Kate's mom said, sitting up and reaching for her phone.

"No, Mom, we need to hide!" Kate whispered loudly.

"Are you sure that's what you saw?" her mom asked, using her most serious mom voice. "One hundred percent sure?"

"Yes. I wouldn't make this up, I swear. He knows I saw it. When I got up off the bag, I begged him to go home, to not do anything. He told me if I told anyone, he would kill me and my family." Big fat tears poured down her face again. "That's why we're hiding."

"Oh my God, Kate." Her mom grabbed her and hugged her hard. "Where is the boy now?"

"I don't know, Mom. He walked toward the buses. That's the last I saw him. I should have come here right away, but I freaked out," Kate said, pulling away.

"Do you know him?"

"No, I don't know him. He's not in my grade. His friends called him Theo."

Her mom called someone on the phone. "Beth! It's me Jackie. I'm in my car in the parking lot. I need you to come out here. It's a real emergency."

Kate felt better being here with her mom.

"No, they aren't alone. Rosie is watching them," Kate's mom continued. "Then leave her there and come out here! This is very, very important, Beth!"

"Beth is my principal. She will know what to do. Here she comes," her mom said, waving to her to get in the back.

"What is going on, Jackie? I enjoy a little cloak and dagger, but I am swamped today. Back-to-back calls all day," Beth elaborated as she got in the back seat.

"Beth, Kate saw a student today at the junior high with a gun in his gym bag. She doesn't know the student. He threatened to kill her and her family if she told. Kate doesn't know where he is, and we don't know what to do."

"What the fuck?" Principal Beth asked. "We need to call the police." She started to dial.

"Wait," Kate shouted. "Stop. If we call the police, he may kill us. That's why we're hiding in here!"

"He might be killing people right now. He might be waiting to open fire at school. The cops will stop him, either arrest him or kill him. He won't kill you. You are safe right here!" Beth was upset. "But you need to tell me everything you know about him."

Kate sighed. "I think his name is Theo."

"If we call the police and they rush to the school with guns out, they could scare him and make him shoot. I mean, if he was shooting people at school, we would know. We need to tell someone smart that will think strategically," Kate's mom said.

"Let's call the Sheriff. Speak to him directly. I know him well. He should pick up." When he didn't, Beth left an urgent voicemail and texted him as well. "While we wait, I have an idea," Beth added.

Beth dialed a number. "Hi Lauren! This is Principal Booker at Carson Elementary. I need your help. This is an emergency. How many Theos do you have there?"

"He's in eighth grade. I don't think he is in my grade," Kate added to be helpful.

"In eighth, don't worry about sixth or seventh," Beth said.

"Just three. Okay great. Would you send me their badge pictures? We're trying to identify a student. This is an emergency and time is crucial," Beth said calmly.

She gave her cell number and hung up.

The three just sat there in silence for a minute.

"Why are we in the car again?" Beth asked.

Before Jackie could respond, Beth's phone rang and everyone jumped.

"This is Beth. Hi, Sheriff! Thanks for calling. We may have a situation on our hands. An emergency. I need you to come to the school right now, Carson Elementary," Beth explained. "A student has a gun in a bag at the middle school and we are not sure where he is. Okay. Yes. We are in the parking lot at Carson. We are trying to find out who the student is." Beth remained calm as she talked to the Sheriff. "I'm with the student who saw the gun and her mother. We're in a car in the parking lot, a red Prius." She placed a hand on Kate's shoulder. "Okay. No sirens. We don't want panic here. The student with the gun is not here."

Beth gave Kate a squeeze. "Okay. We're waiting," Beth said. As she hung up, she said, "I am getting texts," looking at her phone. "Do any of these boys look like Theo?"

Beth handed the phone to Kate.

Kate scrolled through the pictures until the right one was staring at her. "This is him. I am sure."

"Theo Mast," Beth said, looking at the photo.

"Damn, you are good at this," Jackie said to Beth.

"Tell me again—why are we in this car, Jackie?" Beth asked.

"Kate thought it best to hide, and I figured if Theo came after Kate or me, at least I am not in the school with the kids," Kate's mom said.

"Does he know you, Kate? Where you live?" Beth asked.

"I doubt he knows anything about me. I never met him or spoke to him before today. But he could find out."

Just then, the Sheriff's car pulled up. He got out of the car and into the Prius.

"What's up?" he asked.

Beth looked at Kate. "Tell the Sheriff exactly what happened."

Kate explained one more time what had happened that morning.

"Did he leave the school?" The Sheriff asked.

"Maybe? He walked toward the bus loading area. It seemed like he was leaving, but he could have gone anywhere."

"Kate identified him. His name is Theo Mast," Beth added.

The sheriff just stared at Kate for a minute, processing the information. "When did you trip on the bag?"

"Like 7:45, before first period." Kate responded.

"That was more than two hours ago," the Sheriff said.

Kate nodded.

"Okay, we haven't had any reports of shootings. Do we know if he is at the school? Where he is?" the Sheriff asked, while looking at the picture on Beth's phone.

"We have no idea where he is," Jackie said.

"Okay, text me that picture. I got this. Stay here," he said, getting out of the car.

Two more cop cars had quietly pulled up beside them while they were talking.

The Sheriff spoke to the officers. They got on radios. The two cars pulled away, and the Sheriff got back into the Prius.

"We'll find him. I agree, lowkey is better. Stay here, together; it's better than going home at this point. We won't let him come here. We will pick him up first," the Sheriff said, holding the door open for them to get out of the car. "You ladies have done good. I am sure this is very scary. We can discuss more details once we locate Theo Mast."

Just then, a voice came over the radio, "We got him, Sheriff. He was walking down Broad Street, a few blocks from his home address. No bag. Should we pick him up?" the voice asked.

"Yes, but be very careful. He could have a weapon," the Sheriff said into his radio. "I'm on my way. Keep me informed." He rushed off to his car.

Kate, her mom, and Principal Beth watched him drive away.

"I hope it's really him and no one gets hurt," Kate's mom added.

Ten minutes later, Kate was sitting in the warmth of Beth's office, along with her mom, waiting for the Sheriff to call.

When Beth's cell rang, they all jumped.

"Hello Sheriff. What happened?" Beth cut to the chase.

She clicked the speaker on.

"We picked up Theo Mast and took him to the station. We are waiting for his parents to arrive. He didn't have a gun with him. We'll take it from here. Conduct an investigation. You all go back to work or go home. It has been a stressful morning. Kate, we will need to get your official statement but not right now. Okay? Just go home. You're safe," he said in a soothing voice.

"Okay," Kate said, even though she felt less than safe.

"Thank you, Sheriff," her mom added. "We're so relieved you got him so fast and no one was hurt."

Kate and her mom went home. They spent the weekend eating comfort food and watching movies. They did not leave the house. "I still feel nervous. Like Theo is out there and angry with me," Kate said every few hours.

"They got him, Kate. He will be charged. He can't hurt you. It will be okay. But in the meantime, we're staying in the house."

The Sheriff called Monday morning. "Theo Mast said he did not have a gun or a bag with a gun at school or at any time. We searched his home. We interviewed many people. We had no evidence to hold him and released him to his parents."

"What? I don't understand," Kate's mom said. "He threatened my daughter with violence. She saw the gun. Why didn't you interview her?"

"If you want to press charges, come down to the station and an officer will take it all down, Jackie. The thing is, Theo Mast said he did talk to Kate. He said she said some strange things to him. He said Kate has a crush on him. They exchanged a few awkward words, and he walked away. He went home because he wasn't feeling well and later headed back to school. That is when we picked him up. We found no guns or a gym bag. This could be a high school kid relationship issue. But if Kate wants to press charges that he threatened her, she's welcome to do so. Unless someone else heard their conversation, it might be hard to do anything about it. She has every right to file a complaint. Now, ladies, I have a lot of work to do," the Sheriff said. "Let's just be happy there was no violence. There was no gun. Just a misunderstanding of some type. I hope you both have a nice day."

Dread filled Kate. They didn't believe her. And what was this story about her having a crush on him? She hadn't even met him until that morning.

Too nervous to go to school, she stayed home. Her mom went to work.

When her mom got home late that afternoon, she explained more. "Look, Kate, I spoke to Beth and we talked to her friend that is an attorney. We went through various scenarios. I guess without the gun, there is no evidence. Unless someone else saw them or heard you speak to Theo Mast, it's his word against yours." Tears rolled down her mom's face.

Kate felt her blood go cold.

"I believe you, baby," her mom said, hugging Kate. "And so does Beth, of course."

How could Kate ever go back to school? Theo might kill her.

"Beth heard they looked through his school records but didn't see any red flags, so I guess that is good," her mom added, trying to sound hopeful.

"No red flags, but he had a gun, probably more than one by the size of the bag," Kate snapped. "I'm not lying. Why would I? I hate that they think I lied, but not him. He has reason to lie! I don't!"

Her mom gave her a sympathetic smile.

"What am I supposed to do now?" Kate asked.

"I guess just go to school. I mean, he won't tell anyone about it. Why would he? If he convinced the police he did not have a gun, there's no reason to draw attention to this or speak to you, Kate."

"Except he could have hidden the guns. He told me if I said anything, he would kill me and my family. He has a gun, maybe multiple guns. I told someone. Several people in fact. He could kill me." Kate felt frantic, like she was drowning or on fire.

"Just breathe, Kate. The police seem calm about it. I doubt he wants to cause more trouble for himself," her mom said.

"Maybe it was a good thing. Maybe he was going to kill a lot of people, kids at school. I saw the guns and stopped him. I helped him make the right decision. He realized what a crazy idea it was, and now he has a second chance," Kate said with a smile, trying to find a bright side.

"Well, that makes you a hero, better yet, a 'shero'! Even if we are the only people that ever know what happened, that is perfectly okay, as long as Theo Mast never shoots anyone," her mom said, also smiling.

Kate went to bed feeling relief. She was a shero.

"Every little thing, is gonna be alright," she hummed to herself as she fell asleep.

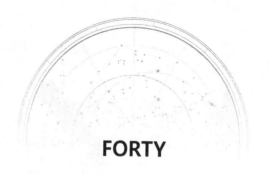

FORTY

Colorado

Kate had been terribly wrong.

As she stepped off the bus, Aislinn, her best friend, ran over to her. "Where have you been?"

"I wasn't feeling well, took a couple of sick days," Kate replied, hugging her friend. "But everything's going to be okay."

"I'm confused, Kate. Were you dating Theo? What happened?" Aislinn asked as they walked to first period.

"What? No, of course not." Kate laughed. "I only ever spoke to him last Friday for like a minute. I didn't even know his name, remember?"

"Theo has been telling his friends that you're stalking him. That you said you loved him, and he said he wasn't interested in you, and you spread some lie about him threatening you with a gun. It's very dramatic. He said you were being really sneaky and scary and weird, and he tried to be nice but finally had to tell the authorities after you threatened him at school last week," Aislinn said quickly. "It's all over. Everyone is talking about it, Kate."

"That is crazy!" Kate said angrily, feeling her cheeks redden. "I'm not into him. I swear."

"I know! I told our friends and my sisters and anyone I hear talking about it that it's not true. But people are like, *why would he make up something so crazy,* and I don't know how to respond. I mean, why would he? It's all so weird." Aislinn popped her gum.

Kate looked around. Was it her imagination or was everyone was staring at her?

"Thanks for telling me, Aislinn. I'll see you at lunch." Kate hugged Aislinn. God, why hadn't she stayed home another day? Why had her mom made her involve the Sheriff? Now she was the laughing stock of school.

Kate's day did not improve.

A few kids directly asked her: "Dude, you stalking Theo?"

Her friends were nicer: "I know he's making it up."

"You are like one of the nicest people at this crappy school," her biology lab partner said. "That Theo kid is delusional. In his dreams."

Others taunted: "Where's your boyfriend?"

Kate thought some of her teachers looked at her, worried, which did not help.

By the time she walked to lunch, she felt exhausted and just looked down so not to see people's curious eyes or encourage remarks or questions. As she entered the cafeteria, Aislinn appeared before her with a tray. "I got your food. Figured you had a rough morning."

"Thanks, Aislinn," Kate said as they sat down.

"Look, Theo made it all up. He totally hates me and wants to make me look bad." Kate clenched and unclenched her fists under the table. "I'm just going to ignore his BS. I know the truth." Kate tried to play it off like she was cool.

"Exactly," Aislinn said, shaking her head. "I mean, I'm going to tell people he is a liar and an asshole. He's lying about my best friend, and he's not going to get away with it." Aislinn bit into her sandwich. "He's a fucking dick."

Better to deal with his lies than a school shooting.

"Hopefully, people will forget about it and move on," Kate added.

But people did not forget or move on.

Every day, there seemed a new element to the story. More stories about crazy, sexual things Kate had said to Theo. Each morning, Aislinn would meet Kate at the bus with some new tidbit that was spreading like wild fire around the school.

By Friday afternoon, Kate was exhausted. She collapsed in bed after school and barely got out of bed all weekend.

On Monday morning, Aislinn greeted her before first. "Ready for what I heard over the weekend?"

"I was in bed all weekend! What could I possibly have done to hurt or scare Theo?" Kate snapped.

"I heard that Theo's parents might ask for you to be removed from school!" Aislinn said.

"What? Why? Can they do that?" Kate was shaken. "This is out of control. Totally out of control." She clenched her fists. "Theo is a fucking dick!"

"Yes. I know," Aislinn said, laughing. "It sounds funny when you swear; it's so rare!"

Kate decided to confront Theo, but for Aislinn's safety, and everyone's else's, she needed to do it alone.

The school was really large, with the different grades in different areas. Kate had only seen Theo twice since the incident: one time walking far away from her near the bus loading area after school, and once across campus outside through a window. Kate wondered why anyone believed his lies since they were never near each other.

Where she could speak to him was the problem.

Kate was sick of the attention, comments, rumors, and lies.

She was frustrated that she couldn't think of a way to get to Theo alone.

It had been seventeen days since she begged Theo to not shoot anyone.

———— ✛ ————

It was cold and sunny as Kate waited for the bus near her house. Despite the sunshine, Kate felt dark and depressed, and the idea of going to school filled her with dread.

She suddenly did something she never did; she started walking down her street. Eventually, she got to a busy street and walked into a fast-food restaurant and ordered a donut. She took a seat and ate it. She enjoyed being anonymous. She felt like a badass for skipping school. There were several old men eating breakfast; some were chatting with each other across tables. There were a few mothers with babies. No one seemed interested in Kate.

Until Theo Mast walked into the restaurant. He didn't see her as he sauntered over to the counter to order, a basketball under one arm.

Kate lifted up her hoodie over her head and slunk down in the booth. Every fiber in her body said flee. Get out of there. She was not ready for the confrontation.

She took several deep breaths. *Calm down. He did not see you,* Kate thought.

He turned around and their eyes locked. He dropped the basketball and almost his tray.

He walked to the closest table, the farthest from her, and put the tray down.

"Get that ball, kid, before someone trips," one of the senior citizens called out good naturedly to him.

Theo quickly collected the ball and sat down with his back to Kate.

"I hope you choke on that breakfast burrito," she whispered to herself.

He suddenly got up, discarded his tray, and walked out the door. Kate jumped up, grabbed her backpack, and ran out after him.

He was fast, and Kate was in an all-out run. This was such a lucky break; she was not going to miss this opportunity to talk to him.

When he got blocked by a red light, Kate caught up.

"What is wrong with you?" Theo panted while he spoke, winded from his sprint.

"I need to talk to you," Kate replied, also gasping for air. "Please, I just need two minutes," Kate pleaded, eyeing the light. If he sprinted again when it turned green, she wasn't sure she could keep up.

"Okay, fine. Say what you want. Fast," Theo said.

"Why? Why did you have a gun that day?" Kate blurted out.

"What gun? I have no idea what you're talking about."

Kate stared at him. "Are you starting to believe your own bullshit? You had a gun, maybe several, in that bag. I saw them. I tripped over them!"

"I have no idea what you're talking about. No idea," he repeated.

Kate squeezed her hands into fists. "Liar," she hissed at him.

"Kate, you're really not helping your situation. If there are cameras on any of these stores, you are on camera following me and freaking out," Theo said, smiling. "Bet I can get a restraining order based on this conversation! We wanted to get one and now we can. You're an idiot."

"You had a gun at school. You were going to kill someone or yourself. There is something seriously wrong with you. You need help," Kate said, angry tears in her eyes.

Theo stopped laughing. "No, Kate, there is something seriously wrong with you. You said you wanted to date me. You said you loved me, and when I rejected you, you freaked out and told the police I had a gun." He shifted positions and leaned down near Kate's ear. "I told you not to tell anyone, but you ran and told the police. But guess what? People believe *me*, not you. You're an idiot. Why would anyone believe a teenage girl? You all love drama and can't control your emotions. Making up lies about a boy that rejected you is pretty typical female behavior," Theo said calmly. "Anyway, my lawyer will be requesting a restraining order."

Theo ran across the street just as the light turned red. Kate walked home, crying.

Theo's lawyer got the restraining order, giving her classmates something new to talk about. Kids that had been making cruel jokes felt justified and were energized to continue doing so. Kids that were quietly curious, now aggressively ignored and shunned her.

Kate's mom was confused. "Kate, we have plans, manuals for school shooting drills. We as teachers and parents think we are prepared, but when it happens, nothing makes sense. Even if he did not have a gun, which I know he did because I completely believe you, everyone should be happy that it was reported and no one was hurt. Shouldn't we all be in this together and grateful it was a mistake? Why all the lies and vitriol?"

"I don't know, Mom. I hate school now. The kids are mean. I can't stand that everyone believes Theo's lies. And I'm afraid of what Theo will do next. Maybe he will bring a gun to school again when things calm down, and then the plans and drills will have to work," Kate replied.

Eight weeks after Kate tripped over Theo's bag, they packed up to move.

As her mom drove down their street for the last time, neither she nor Kate looked back.

"You saved people's lives. You did the right thing. Don't ever forget that. Kate, you were honest and so brave. You are so brave," she said, looking at Kate.

FORTY-ONE

Forty-Seven Days After the Shooting

Kate knew telling the truth was dangerous. Kate knew if these people chose not to believe her, it was game over. She would lose her job for sure, maybe go to prison, maybe worse. And unlike before, she couldn't just move to Florida to avoid the mess.

She leaned over, put her head in her hands, and started to speak loudly to be sure the mask did not muffle her words.

She told the whole story. She began when she was running on the trail and the mass shooting happened. She told them about Rex and the warnings and the email to her boss, Carol. She told them how she tried to communicate with leadership by doing the bare minimum and hoped that was enough. She told them everything.

She sat straight up and sighed loudly, looking around the room.

All eyes were riveted to her face, making her feel self-conscious.

"Shoot, I've been touching my face," Kate said, looking at her hands. She pulled sanitizer from her pocket. "Anyway, Rex said I must 'tell the leaders at Space Force to clean up the pollution, the dangerous garbage, now.' He said that if I didn't do as I was told, there'd 'be more violence.' Rex said I 'had five days,' and we are running out of time.

The fear of more violence made her feel bolder. She looked directly, one by one, into every set of eyes around the table.

No one said a word.

"I've done my part. I've told you everything I know. I followed Rex's orders. Now the ball is in your hands. I'll be leaving," Kate said, starting to stand. "Sorry to dump all this heavy and scary information on you. I know it's a lot to process, but I have faith you'll do the right thing."

Do I have faith that this room of acting leaders will take the actions to forestall doom?

"I know I did not like having this dumped on me. We live in such crazy and scary times," Kate added with sincerity.

"Hold on now," Acting General Someone said. "We have a lot of questions."

"Yes. Like where is this Rex guy?" asked another officer. "And how do we find him? Has someone taken her phone, analyzed her talk and text data?"

"I don't know how to find him. I never actively sought him out. I told you everything I know about him. He reached out to me. I don't know why or who he is or how to reach him," she said.

"What does Rex mean? Maybe it stands for something?" The youngest officer said to the room. "Maybe he's North Korean? We still don't know what happened there, and they don't have a lot of guns. Same with China—way more people than guns."

"Rex is the link. We must find him," the Acting General said, looking at Kate.

"Once again, I think Rex is an avatar of some kind. Like I said, he changed forms. At one point he was a large orange cat, and it reminded me of a cat I fostered named Rex. That's why I call him Rex. He, or it, never offered me his/its real name." Kate crossed her arms across her chest.

No wonder bureaucrats are inefficient. They don't listen.

"And frankly, all this clamoring to find Rex? It doesn't matter. Rex does not matter. Whatever or wherever he is, he caused a worldwide mass shooting that killed hundreds of millions of people. It wants the garbage cleaned up in space or there will be more violence. You have a few days to stop more violence," Kate said. "I'm not a general or leadership here, but it's clear to me that you'd be better off spending your time organizing a mass cleanup. Get the most intelligent people in the world together to locate the garbage and create a plan to collect it. Call all current and former astronauts together from all over the world and get them into space!"

"Just like in the movies," the young officer added snidely.

"That is not going to happen, Kate. There is so much debris up there now. How would we even catch it? Some of it moves at incredibly high speeds; it's dangerous to our satellites and space crafts. Even if we could do it, it would cost billions, maybe trillions of dollars to collect it and, what, bring it back to Earth? And what? Put it in the recycle bin? That is just crazy," the Acting General said.

"So, what I'm saying is crazy? That cleaning up our mess to save humanity is just crazy?" Kate said, standing up.

Everyone in the room looked down, avoiding eye contact with her. "No. You are all crazy. Rex killed hundreds of millions of people. The mass shooting has destroyed people, families, whole communities. The shooting destroyed our economy, which was already a mess from the pandemic. The news says we may have food shortages this winter, or not, since there are way less people to feed. We are living in this new bizarre, horrific world with heartbreak and loss and fear that is uncalculatable; yet you say we can't clean up our mess because it's too expensive?" Kate shouted, feeling the anger and frustration build in her. Not just anger over her current situation, but the pandemic, Colorado, all of it.

"And it's not like this has not happened before. Over and over and over we destroy everything. Our oceans are polluted with plastics, killing fish, birds, whales, everything. We have polluted our atmosphere with global warming gasses. There is not a spring, river, lagoon or pond that is not full of pesticides, fertilizers, oil, and human shit. We pollute and kill everything we touch. The only difference is nature works slower. We were warned for decades about global warming and extreme weather and zoonotic diseases, and WE HAVE DONE NOTHING. This time it's fast and targeted. Clean up your garbage or die," Kate said and slammed her fists on the table, just like the acting general.

The room was silent for a minute.

"Yes, Kate, that is why we must get to Rex and stop him," the General said.

"Oh my God," Kate exclaimed in frustration. "You guys don't get it. You're so busy war mongering with Rex that you really can't see the answer is right in front of you."

"We get what you're saying, but as noted, a cleanup of that scale will take time. It'll take money. Innovation. We have to come up with new technology. This can't happen overnight. We would need to get Congress involved. What we need now is Rex," the General replied.

"Oh my God! The mass shooting was unimaginable. How it occurred is incomprehensible. If Rex was responsible, he has mind-blowing intelligence or superpowers, and you think you can find him and stop him? What are you going to do—shoot him?" Kate yelled. "And with what, a gun?"

Kate took a few deep breaths, calming herself down.

"I've done my part. You all have a lot of work to do in a very short amount of time, so I will leave you to it," Kate said, stomping to the door and trying the doorknob, surprised it was unlocked. No one stopped her from walking out.

FORTY-TWO

Forty-Seven Days After the Shooting

K ate walked down the hall and toward the main entrance; it looked like they weren't going to hold or arrest her. Whatever they did was on them now.

Parked illegally in front of the building was Sinclair. He rolled down the passenger window. "Come on, Kate. Get in."

"How did you know I was here?" Kate asked as she climbed in the front seat.

"I followed you," Sinclair said, pulling away from Space Force. "Frankly, I'm surprised you're out. I had images of them taking you to the Pentagon or away in a helicopter or just plain jail." He glanced at Kate's face. "Are you okay? You look okay. No torture?'

Kate exhaled heavily. "I'm totally fine. They didn't torture me. They just asked me lots of questions. I repeated the same Rex story I told you. They were frustrated and didn't like it. They did not like that I don't know how to get to Rex."

"Huh," Sinclair said, signaling and moving over a lane.

"They are very focused on Rex. Think if they can get to him, they can arrest the mastermind of the mass shooting and get on with life," Kate explained. "Apparently, I am the thing, the person, blocking the world from being safe and going back to normal. They won't accept that I am just the messenger."

"But here you are. They can't see you as that much of an impediment or they wouldn't have let you walk," he said.

"Where are we going?" Kate asked. Not home, from the looks of the road he turned on.

"I kind of figured they'd follow us," Sinclair said, glancing at the rearview mirror. "But I'm not trained in evading federal agents, so who knows."

He smiled at Kate. She felt her shoulders relax. She wasn't in jail. She needed to call Kyle.

"I'm happy you are okay, really happy. I was worried. All kinds of crazy things going through my mind. Clearly, I watch too many movies," he added.

"I think they can just track my phone," Kate said, looking at her phone, scrolling through the many worried messages from Kyle and her mom. "My mom must have seen me on the news. I have like a dozen texts and calls from her. I better call her."

Kate hated to think she was causing her mom stress.

"Wait, Kate, we really need to talk. I'm not sure what will happen next, so let's talk, and then you can call everyone," he said.

"Okay, sure," Kate replied.

"But first things first." Sinclair parked the car and jumped out. "Wait here."

"What? Where are you going?" Kate asked.

"Just trust me. Wait here. I'll be back."

Kate watched him jog away and decided she needed to call her mother, despite what she agreed to with Sinclair.

"Mom, hey I am okay. Things are crazy, but I am safe," Kate said as soon as her mom picked up.

"Are you sure, Kate? I saw you on the news. They said you are a person of interest. What does that even mean?" Her mom sounded both concerned and relieved.

"Yes, totally okay. There was some mix-up. Someone said something scary to me, and I told Space Force management. They decided I know more than I'm letting on and that I'm potentially involved."

"What?" her mom asked.

Kate laughed. "I know. Sound familiar? Jeez Louise, history does repeat itself."

"Where are you?"

"Downtown with a friend who is helping me sort out this nightmare. He's coming back now. Let me call you back when I get home. I'll tell you the whole crazy story," Kate said, watching Sinclair walk back to the car.

"Okay. Sounds good. Love you, Kate."

"Love you too, Mom," Kate said as she hung up.

"I figured you might be hungry," Sinclair said, getting in the car.

"Let's go eat in Rock Creek Park, far from cameras and recording devices," he said pulling away. "I have to tell you a story."

A few minutes later, they were sitting at a picnic table far enough from the car, their phones, or any structures that might have cameras.

"One vegan grains and greens bowl," Sinclair said, opening her container. "One vegetarian bowl for me. I love cheese."

Kate ate the entire bowl in five minutes flat. "Didn't realize how hungry I was. Thanks for dinner, Sinclair," Kate said.

"My pleasure," he said, eating at a reasonable pace. "You know, Yvette and I were splitting up. We would probably have been divorced by the end of the pandemic."

"Oh no! Was it a pandemic split? Just too much time together? I have heard of so many couples splitting due to this damn disease. I am so sorry…" Kate's voice trailed off.

"She's dead, Kate. It doesn't matter now. And I'm telling you this for a reason."

The moon was out and huge, and Kate waived away mosquitoes as Sinclair talked.

"We met in college. We were scientists and had so much in common. It was like we were made for each other; we both loved physics and space. We went to grad school together, got our doctorates, and worked for NASA. We were living our dreams. It was fantastic. Yvette loved the engineering part of space exploration. She was all about the launches. She started in Brevard and followed the satellite and research launches. I moved with her and did my research. NASA was pretty flexible with us."

Kate wished she'd gotten to know Yvette; she sounded like a cool person.

"Over the past couple of years, Yvette became more interested in what corporate space was up to. She would work with the billionaire titans of space exploration on the side. She always knew more about what was happening than NASA did. She said she would be leaving NASA soon for a sweet, sweet deal. She was very excited, said we would be rolling in dough as well as doing what we love. Living the dream, especially for a little girl from Detroit. She was so excited," Sinclair said, suddenly looking very sad.

Kate squeezed his hand with compassion and encouragement. She figured if either had COVID, they had probably infected the other by now.

"Anyway," Sinclair continued, "the new gig was in Brevard and she was excited to move back to Florida. She just assumed I'd be okay with it. I had loved living in Satellite Beach years ago, loved working at Kennedy Space Center, but no way was I going back. Brevard County has become so racist, I can't even stand to visit friends there. It's become worse with this President, making public racism cool again. I felt scared just driving to the beach. With so many confederate flags, I could not imagine living there. Especially after six years here. Say what you want about D.C., but it's not a racist city."

"So, you were going to stay here, and Yvette was going to move to Florida? That's why you decided to separate?" Kate asked.

"Yes, that and some other stuff. Yvette didn't want kids. She grew up with a lot of brothers and sisters, chaos, dysfunction. Yvette was all business and very career driven. I was never sure what I wanted. I mean, I love my job, just not sure if that was all I want," Sinclair said, taking a big swig of water.

Kate wasn't sure about having kids either. Not in this world.

"When the pandemic started and we locked down, I dragged the telescope up to the roof. Put some equipment in the back yard. There were several wonderful celestial events to watch and entertain and inspire. I thought Yvette and I could reconnect over what we love, maybe even each other. Make something good come out of this nightmare, but Yvette had no interest. She kept traveling for her rich gods, taking risks, staying focused on work and the prize." Sinclair cleared his throat.

Was he getting choked up?

"Wow, I'm really sorry to dump all this on you," he said, shaking his head.

"What, why sorry?" She had gotten caught up in the story. "You're mourning. Talking about the person and the loss is part of the process. It's especially important now since we are all so isolated."

"We're not here to talk about my break-up with my deceased wife. That's a sad story on top of a sad story and requires a beverage stronger than water. We're here to discuss stopping violence," he said.

Kate nodded. *Finally, someone who made sense. Too bad he hadn't been in that room at Space Force.*

"My wife was very involved with launches. She tracked and attended dozens of launches every year. Early last year, she said there had been a major collision way up high. She said NASA and corporate space were on alert to find out which satellites may have been lost. She said the explosion was so big, it put everyone on alert that it might trigger chain reaction collisions. They wanted to know what was lost, what replacements would need to be launched, and, of course, who would get the business. After a few months of excited chatter, Yvette went quiet on the topic. I asked a couple of times if they found out what hit what, but she would just shrug like it was old news."

Could this be what Rex is so upset about?

"This struck me as odd and not like Yvette at all. I actually thought there must be an angle; something was up for her to just drop a topic without resolution. It had made the press. There was lots of interest and talk and then silence," Sinclair said, taking a sip of water.

"Over the past few days, I dug into Yvette's work, looking for pictures, evidence of the explosion. She brought a lot of work home to avoid the appearance of a conflict of interest. I was thinking, that accident may have created some new garbage, some new dangerous pollution."

"Did it?" Kate asked.

"I don't know yet, but I have a few leads," Sinclair said.

Kate absorbed his words. "Huh. Interesting. But I fear we are heading down a similar rabbit hole as Space Force. They want Rex. They think if they get Rex, they stop him and future violence without bending to Rex's terms. I know they can't stop him. What we need is to create a plan to clean up the garbage, the dangerous pollution."

"Yes. True. But Kate, we have just 24 hours and can't even create a plan to clean up the garbage in that amount of time. I'm just trying to figure out what caused this mess. Why now? Why did Rex cause the mass shooting? If we can figure out why he did it, it might just buy us some time for sanity to prevail at Space Force and NASA," Sinclair said. "I don't know. Maybe this sounds just as frustrating to you as what you heard from Space Force."

Kate was suddenly beaming at Sinclair.

"Why are you so happy," he laughed at Kate's sudden change of mood.

"You believe me. You believe all of it. You have a better grasp on this mess than anyone. I'm so happy you are here with me, helping me," she said, happy tears in her eyes. "This has been the longest day ever. A very strange day. I am exhausted, even though I took like a really long nap earlier. The stress has wiped me out. Your idea sounds good, but I can barely think." She wiped the tears away.

They stood up, collected their trash, and started walking to the car.

"You know, I was just thinking back to something Rex said," Kate said.

"What did he say, Kate?" Sinclair asked.

"'*And you know a biophysicist.*' He said it as he changed into you. It's like he knew you would help me."

Sinclair stopped walking. "He changed into me? Rex changed into me?"

"Yes, I forgot about it until just now. It didn't seem as important as the warnings about violence. Let's go. I am really tired, and Kyle must be worried sick," Kate said, getting in the car.

They drove the short distance home without speaking until Kate broke the silence. "Rex said it at the end of our last encounter. He called me brave and then said, '*and you know a biophysicist*.' The biophysicist comment makes sense, not sure about the brave remark. I have no idea how Jo-Ellen knew about it. She mentioned it earlier at the Space Force interview."

As they pulled up in front of Sinclair's house, Kate got out of the car. "Thank you, Sinclair, for picking me up and dinner and believing me and helping. I can't thank you enough."

Sinclair jumped out of the car. "Wait, Kate. Why did Rex call you brave, and what do you mean Jo-Ellen mentioned it?"

"Kate!" Kyle shouted from across the street.

He must have been watching for Sinclair's car.

"Kate, where have you been? What happened? Come home," Kyle urgently called.

"Good night, Sinclair," Kate said as she walked quickly to her house and embraced Kyle on the porch.

"I am so tired, Kyle. I will tell you everything tomorrow. I just need sleep now."

FORTY-THREE

Forty-Eight Days after the Shooting

Kate woke up early, sat cross-legged on the living room floor, and closed her eyes for some slow, deep breaths. She hadn't meditated in days and wanted to regain a positive, peaceful outlook to ground her for whatever was going to happen next. She tried to wipe her mind clear of worries about Rex and Space Force and dangerous pollution and the negative narrative that she was not handling this well. Instead, she thought about images of beaches and nature and beauty. She smiled remembering a time when she was snorkeling and a pod of dolphins swam under her. She focused on the tropical flowers and wildlife she loved in Florida as she took long inhales and soothing exhales.

Assault weapons and bodies kept creeping in.

No. She wanted sea turtles and sunsets.

Guns littering the streets. Nuclear warheads pointed all over the world.

No. Baby manatees and white sand beaches.

She filled her lungs with air. "There is nothing I can do about anything now," she said as she exhaled. "I've done all I can to prevent more violence."

Inhale. Exhale. "I have done everything Rex asked, fulfilling my commitment. I have honored you, Rex."

"Who is Rex?" Kyle asked loudly.

Kate jumped. "What the hell, Kyle! I'm meditating!"

"Sorry!" Kyle exclaimed. "But who in the hell is Rex, and why are you honoring him?"

Kate got up and stretched. "The nutbag in the park. I think his name is Rex. I also think I told you that," Kate said, annoyed that he'd interrupted her moments at attempted peace of mind. "I've had a terrible week. I did not sleep well. I really needed that meditation. Now I really need a shower." Kate headed to the bathroom.

"Sorry, babe!" Kyle called after her. "But over breakfast, you're telling me everything, starting with what happened yesterday. I'll make a great breakfast: vanilla oat milk kale blueberry smoothies and veg sausage."

"Sounds wonderful!" Kate yelled over her shoulder, pleased with herself that she distracted him away from Rex again.

She did not want to lie to Kyle.

FORTY-FOUR

Forty-Eight Days After the Shooting

As far as Kate knew, she still had a job. After her shower and a delicious breakfast, she sat down on the couch to work. She told Kyle the bare minimum.

Her inbox was full of dozens of emails with questions from colleagues, clients, and even her boss wanting to know what was up. Most included similar subject lines: I SAW YOU ON CNN or PERSON OF INTEREST????

It was weird that they did not freeze her out of her account. *Unless they are monitoring me through it?* She snapped the computer shut.

"Guess I am not working today," Kate shouted to the kitchen, where Kyle was stationed at the table.

She paced around before finding her notebook and pen and started writing down the events from the previous day. When and how she got to Space Force, questions they asked, Sinclair's story. She needed to write it down to process it, and she hoped, help her decide what the hell to do next.

Kyle clicked on the TV, startling her back to reality.

"I don't want to watch TV, Kyle," Kate complained. There went her peace of mind.

"Well, I can't focus because every other minute I get a text or email asking why you're a person of interest and what is going on," Kyle replied, watching the TV. "Plus, constant news alerts from the newspaper and CNN."

"That is why I left my phone upstairs and shut my laptop. It's insane, nonstop, distracting, and not helping anything." She glanced at the TV and saw her image and "person of interest" scroll across the screen. "They questioned me and let me go. I should not be a person of interest anymore."

"Guess you'll be a person of interest until they find someone else of interest," Kyle replied.

"Turn it off, Kyle! Seriously, it's not helping anything. It's just stressing me out."

When he did not, Kate ran upstairs with her notebook. She flopped on the bed, landing on her phone. Without looking at it, she stuck it in her pocket and focused on her notepad.

She heard loud pounding on the front door.

"What now?" she called downstairs to Kyle.

"Bunch of news crews and people out front, Kate. Seems like they want in the house. They aren't here for me; I can tell you that," Kyle yelled upstairs, sounding stressed.

Kate fussed with her hair and applied sunblock. She was stalling for time. She was confident reporters couldn't come in, but cops or FBI could if they had a warrant. Who knew what Space Force was saying about her now?

"Kate! Come down! This is crazy! You have to see this!" Kyle shouted nervously.

Kate went downstairs.

As she hit the bottom step, Kyle explained, "I went in the kitchen so they couldn't see me. Some reporters were looking through the front window. And in just like two minutes, it changed from a few people on the porch to this." Kyle pulled back the curtain and revealed dozens of excited people squishing their faces to the window. Some held ID's or signs saying what network they were with. They were pushing and jostling each other to get Kate's attention and all shouting at once.

Kyle closed the curtain.

"Oh my God!" Kate said, looking at Kyle.

"That is a lot of reporters. Okay, reporters can't get in the house. If it's cops or FBI or Space Force, they can clear a path, so it's just clickbait thirsty reporters. Can we call the police on them? Were they wearing masks?" Kate asked as they walked to the kitchen and away from the hum of voices asking them to come out, demanding they answer questions.

There was a smash and breaking glass. They both turned around as something hit the living room floor. Someone had thrown an object hard enough to smash the glass window.

"I don't think they're all reporters. Let's get out of here," Kate said, rushing to the back door.

They walked out the back door and saw over their chain fence that the alley was full of people.

"Weird that they're breaking into our house through the front but won't jump the four-foot fence?" Kyle said as he grabbed Kate's hand and ran left.

"We still have the 'Beware of Dog' sign up from when we had Barney," Kate noted.

They jumped neighbors' fences and ran low, bobbing and weaving through their small back yards until they got to the end of the block. People started chasing them, running fast down the alley.

A car horn beeped and they looked up. Sinclair was across the street at the corner in his car.

"We can't make it. They'll cut us off!" Kate said.

"Hide here," Kyle said, pushing Kate into a wood pile behind the steps of the house in the yard they were hiding in. "I'll distract them."

"No way! Those aren't all reporters. That's a mob!" Kate whispered loudly.

But Kyle bounded out, jumped over the last fence, and was on the street with his hands in the air. "Okay, I'll take a few questions," he shouted, acting like it was just a mass of unruly reporters.

He then ran to the right, heading back to the front of the house.

The alley mob chased after him, and Kate could hear people shouting: "There he is! Kate's boyfriend!"

Kate crept out quietly, jumped the final fence, and ran to Sinclair's car. She didn't look up or behind her as she got in and they drove off.

"Oh my God. Did you see that?" Kate asked Sinclair. "They'll rip Kyle apart! Especially when they realize I'm not there."

"There are a lot of cameras. Reporters from all the major channels: CNN, ABC, FOX. Too many cameras to hurt him, though they are getting out of control. I was watching from my porch. I called you both a few times to warn you as the trucks pulled stealthily on the street, not right in front of your house. Things escalated so quickly. That's not just reporters. I also called the police. This is my street too. You didn't answer your phone," Sinclair explained, fast and jumbled as he drove.

"No, our phones were blowing up, so we decided to ignore them. Obviously, not a good idea," she said.

Sirens and police cars whizzed past them, heading to the house.

"I hope Kyle is okay," Kate said, imagining the worst. "I think maybe we should go to Space Force? Have them arrange a press conference? Something sane and controlled and professional to get that mob off us." Kate tried to pull herself together. "They caused this mess; they should fix it."

"I think it is too late for that. Those reporters want blood. It was all over the news this morning. You, or your partner, Rex, caused the mass shooting or know who did and are not saying. The corrupt news is running it that way. Conspiracy theories are being presented as facts. People are hysterical, saying you killed their loved ones. Some people were saying you should be shot. It's really bad," he explained, driving too fast for Kate's comfort. "And the worst part—"

"Is that we left Kyle back there! They might be hurting him!" Kate yelled as Sinclair's words sank in.

"No, I think Kyle will be okay. They might assume he's in the dark because some are saying Rex is your secret lover. Plus, cops were heading there, so hopefully he is okay," Sinclair said. "The worst part now is the news not mentioning Space Force. Only thing I saw was that Space Force had put you on administrative leave without pay and might let you go if it's determined you had anything to do with the shooting. It's like they're distancing themselves from you. Cutting you off, letting you take the heat alone," he said.

"Like Jo-Ellen warned us," Kate replied. "So, what do we do? Where do we go?"

"How about a road trip to the Eastern shore of Virginia? We need to find out what NASA knows about that mysterious collision. We need some answers," Sinclair said, looking at Kate.

FORTY-FIVE

Forty-Eight Days After the Shooting

They drove awhile in silence.

Kate kept dialing Kyle's phone and sending texts, but she got no response. "Where are we going exactly?" she finally asked.

"I have a friend, or I should say Yvette had a friend, at Goddard Space Center. Specifically, she is with Wallops Flight Facility on the coast. They send off interplanetary and International Space Station missions from there. Her name comes up in the notes I found in Yvette's computer about the collision."

"Oh."

"Listen to this, Kate. I made this call last night. I have Yvette's phone and password and I've been looking into her contacts. This guy and Yvette communicated constantly. I recorded our call."

Sinclair pushed play and handed the phone to Kate.

"I know this is not Yvette, but Yvette's phone, so I'm hoping this is Sinclair," a man's voice said suspiciously, in a loud whisper.

"Yes, hi, Jack. How are you?"

"Is this who I think it is?" Kate asked, hearing the distinct California surfer voice.

Sinclair nodded yes.

"Hey Sinclair! I'm okay, all things considered. This fucking pandemic sucks. It sucks so much. I miss Yvette so much. I miss her every single day. Why did she have a gun? We had so many plans. I am really lucky I did not own a gun. I have in the past, but not now. I might have some at my other houses. I don't know. I have a lot of things," Jack said.

"Is he drunk?" Kate asked. Sinclair did not respond, just focused on driving in silence.

Kate couldn't believe Sinclair was just chatting with one of the richest men in the world. Space was not this billionaire's only interest.

"I was devastated to hear about Yvette. I adored her. She was brilliant and professional and I miss her every single day. Dude, I had a condolences card sent. Did you get it? I'm sure you received hundreds. But this doesn't matter. How are you, Sinclair?"

"I'm okay. Hanging in there. Wish I had convinced her to get rid of that revolver."

Kate felt tears welling up, hearing Sinclair discuss Yvette's death with someone for the first time. It sounded a little prepared, like he created this generic response for calls like this one; it must still be very hard.

"*Jack, I know you are a busy man so I'm going to cut to the chase. I'm going through some of Yvette's work, and I have some questions.*"

Jack took a deep breath. "*Look Sinclair, I'm not sure how much you knew. Yvette was going to be my VP of launches. She was going to move over here to my company, leave NASA. I was going to set her up on the beach in Florida. We were going to change the trajectory of space exploration. We had so many plans. So much work had been done. We were going to change the world.*"

"Is he crying?" Kate asked. "He's definitely drunk."

Sinclair nodded.

"*Yes, I know, Jack. She was very excited about the opportunity,*" Sinclair said on the recording.

Kate wondered if this relationship had not put Sinclair and Yvette on the fast track to divorce. He had said there was no way he was moving to Florida.

"*Jack, I do know that some of Yvette's work may have been, let's say, a conflict of interest, but I honestly don't care. I do know you know a lot. You know what corporate space is up to, as well as NASA. And I just have a question about that big collision that happened last year. It was all over the news, and then it went quiet. Just curious if anything new has happened since Yvette passed. I haven't been paying attention, and Yvette, of course, had her ear on everything,*" Sinclair said.

"*Yes, I figured NASA or Yvette brought you in on that. I mean you are a biophysicist who studies things brought back from space, right? That is how Yvette explained you. What did they find? Yvette was obsessed with the collision, both because of all the damage and preventing that from happening to my equipment. So, like, what caused it? Was it a new metal or mineral? Dude, did you find carbon? Wait, was it just our stuff mismanaged? A cover-up either way maybe? So much damage. Very expensive damage, I bet. I figured she would let me know when she knew. What did they find?"* Jack asked excitedly.

There was a long pause on the recording. Kate glanced at Sinclair, but he was staring at the road ahead.

"Whatever it is, wherever it is, if you share that information with me, I can offer you the same deal I had with Yvette. Welcome to my world, Sinclair! The sky is the limit!" Jack laughed. *"Or not! The sky is clearly not the limit!"*

Jack kept laughing loudly.

Kate wondered if he was on drugs as well as drunk.

"Also, Sinclair, there's buzz about someone at Space Force knowing what caused the mass shooting, beyond what is in the media. Isn't that interesting? Let's find out what is really going on. Okay, buddy? Let's work together," Jack said.

"Okay, will do, Jack. Good night," Sinclair said, hanging up the phone.

"He seemed drunk, high, and every bit the egomaniac they say he is." Kate swiped the recording away and put Yvette's phone down. She wondered if Jack and Yvette had been sleeping together. "The mysterious collision must be involved. Too much secrecy," Kate said, figuring that is what Sinclair was thinking.

Her phone rang and she jumped, startled. "Kyle, thank God! Are you okay?" Kate said into the phone.

"Yes. Now, anyway. It was crazy for a few minutes. I was literally running down our street at top speed, bobbing and weaving around the reporters and nutbags yelling for you. It was terrifying, Kate. I am so glad you weren't there. People grabbed my shirt and pulled me. I ran as fast as I could toward downtown. Anyway, some police showed up, and the crowd stopped chasing me. A cop car cut me off and I got in. The police were great. Took me to the station for safety. They asked a ton of questions. I told them what I knew. Anyway, I'm sitting outside a coffee shop now across from the station. They, some of the cops, went to clear the street and house. They'll let me know when it's safe to go home," Kyle said in an excited rush.

"But you're okay, right?" Kate asked.

"Yes. Totally fine now," Kyle said.

"I am so happy you're safe! I was so worried! Kyle, you were so brave this morning to lead that insane mob away! I can't thank you enough, baby," Kate said, tears in her eyes.

"It's okay, Kate. Wait, where are you? Are you safe?" Kyle demanded.

"Yes. I'm with Sinclair. We have an idea. It's probably a crazy long shot, so please don't tell anyone. I don't want anyone to get excited," Kate said.

Sinclair gave her a worried look. He shook his head indicating she should not say anything.

"What is it?" Kyle asked.

"We might know where Rex might be. It's just a guess, but at this point, better than nothing."

"Okay, that's cool. Where do you think he is?" Kyle asked.

"Sinclair has been looking into infamous space junkies that have been social media conspiracy enthusiasts. He thinks he knows of one in New York, seems similar to Rex. It's complicated. We are heading to New York now." She looked at Sinclair. He gave a thumbs up, acknowledging her lie. "I'd really rather not say anything else. If we're wrong, we could be bringing unfair and hostile attention to an innocent person."

"Okay, I guess. Be careful, babe," Kyle said.

"Can I call you when we get there? When I know more?" Kate asked.

I don't want to lie to him more. He may have saved my life.

"Okay. Call me later. I love you, Kate."

"Kyle, promise me, you won't tell anyone what we are doing or where we are heading, okay? Not the cops or reporters or anyone?" Kate asked.

Sinclair was smart to have her keep their true plans from Kyle. The less he knew, the better.

"I won't tell a soul, but Kate, the police are being really cool. They want to speak to you. They said they have no grounds to arrest you; they just want to talk. I hate that you don't trust them, Ms. BLM," Kyle said a little snidely.

"I do trust them. Some of them anyway and certainly the ones that helped you today," Kate added, frustrated that they were having this conversation now. "I will call you when I know more. I love you."

Kate hung up, and they sat in silence for a few minutes.

"It was smart not to tell him. He'd tell someone, thinking he was helping," Kate said to Sinclair, trying to convince herself lying was okay. "He won't understand why we're heading to Goddard Space Center or Wallops, and it would be a whole long conversation."

"That all makes sense, Kate," Sinclair said.

He took his eyes off the road to look at Kate. "You want to know why? Why I'm risking my career, maybe my life, to help you?"

Kate felt the intensity of his gaze, gestured with her chin for him to take his eyes back to the road. "Yeah, now that you mention it? Why?"

"Kate, I've worked my whole life looking for signs of life in space, hoping for the chance to meet someone like Rex, if he is what we think he is. My research indicated it was possible, but I never thought I'd get this close. Whatever happens, I'm happy you reached out to me. That we're doing this together."

He really does believe all of it. He believes me. Kate felt a brief wave of relief, quickly followed by a rush of anxiety.

"How long until we get there?" Kate asked.

"Another hour or so," Sinclair responded.

"At least this road trip will distract us, even if we find nothing. It beats sitting around and waiting," Kate said.

"Waiting for the reporters or mob to rip you apart? Or for the police or FBI to arrest you?" Sinclair asked, confused.

"I was referring to more violence. We passed the deadline," Kate said, looking out the window and up at the sky.

The End of the First Book in The Impact Series

Author Bio:

C K Westbrook is an environmentalist who lives and works in Washington D.C. and is a self-described old school news junkie. Since the state of our planet and the news are bleak and depressing, Westbrook escapes reality by creating intriguing characters in a science fiction world. The world these characters live in may also be dark and scary, but they do have fantastic adventures that impact their planet. In addition to creating imaginative stories, Westbrook literally breaks free from daily life with an intense passion for travel and has been to all seven continents. Westbrook loves weaving real world topics and crises into suspenseful sci-fi and fantasy. To learn more about CK Westbrook, please go to www.ckwestbrook.com.

Ready for more Kate, Kyle, and Sinclair action and suspense? The Collision, book two of The Impact Series, will be published in fall 2022.

MORE BOOKS FROM
4 HORSEMEN PUBLICATIONS

FANTASY, SCIFI, & PARANORMAL ROMANCE

VALERIE WILLIS
Cedric: The Demonic Knight
Romasanta: Father of
Werewolves
The Oracle: Keeper of the
Gaea's Gate

Artemis: Eye of Gaea
King Incubus: A New Reign

V.C. WILLIS
Prince's Priest
Priest's Assassin

HORROR, THRILLER, & SUSPENSE

AMANDA BYRD
sdfasd

MARIA DEVIVO
Witch of the Black Circle
Witch of the Red Thorn

ERIKA LANCE
Jimmy
Illusions of Happiness
No Place for Happiness
I Hunt You

MARK TARRANT
The Death Riders
Howl of the Windigo
Guts and Garter Belts

DISCOVER MORE AT
4HORSEMENPUBLICATIONS.COM

CPSIA information can be obtained
at www.ICGtesting.com
Printed in the USA
BVHW030836220322
631480BV00013B/12